AN ACCIDENTAL CORPSE

HELEN A. HARRISON

PUBLISHED BY DUNEMERE BOOKS

DUNEMERE
Books

This is a work of fiction, in which historical figures and invented
characters interact. Some of the events described actually happened;
others are pure fantasy, products of the author's imagination.

Publisher's Cataloging-in-Publication data
Names: Harrison, Helen A. (Helen Amy), author.
Title: An Accidental corpse / Helen A. Harrison.
Series: The Corpse Trilogy.
Description: New York, NY: Dunemere Books, 2018.
Identifiers: ISBN 978-1-947936-05-8
Subjects: LCSH Pollock, Jackson, 1912-1956—Fiction.
| Pollock, Jackson, 1912-1956—Friends and associates—Fiction. |
Artists—Fiction. | Murder—Investigation—Fiction. | East Hampton
(N.Y.)—Fiction. | Detective and mystery fiction. | BISAC FICTION
/ Mystery & Detective / General Classification: LCC PS3608.A78345
A23 2018 | DDC 813.6--dc23

ISBN: 978-1-947936-05-8

To Roy
Always

ONE.

Saturday, August 11, 1956

By eleven o'clock on a hot, muggy morning, when the Fitzgerald family arrived at the Fishermen's Fair in Springs, the crowd had filled the grounds of Ashawagh Hall and was spilling onto Parsons Place and Amagansett Road, which were cordoned off with snow fencing. With its display of handmade crafts, tables laden with baked goods, preserves, and other local delicacies, children's rides and games, and an exhibition of reasonably priced works by many of the well-known artists who lived in the area, the fair was the acme of the East Hampton hamlet's summer season.

Fireplace Road was already lined with parked cars. Fitz was waved on by a local uniform and had to park nearly a quarter mile north of the fairgrounds. *Not so bad*, he thought as he opened the car door for his wife, Nita, and their eight-year-old son, TJ. *A bit humid, but it sure beats the steamy city. When I was a beat cop I used to dread days like this. By the time I finished my rounds I'd be sweating like a pig.*

In the thirteen years since Brian Fitzgerald and Juanita Diaz had tied the knot, this was their first real family vacation. For the first couple of years they'd take off from their duties as New York City police officers for a week in a Rockaway Beach boardinghouse. As their careers advanced—his to sergeant, then captain; hers to detective—they spent their holidays studying for exams and doing the volunteer work that earned brownie points with the promotions board.

Now they felt they'd earned a two-week stay at the Sea Spray Inn in East Hampton, a charming beachfront resort with a string of reasonably priced housekeeping cottages adjacent to the main building. They could come and go as they pleased and economize by cooking most meals for themselves. Plus TJ could have his own room. The town had a convenient Long Island Rail Road connection to Pennsylvania Station, but Fitz's father had told them to forget about the train and lent them his Chevy coupe for the duration. If they got tired of the beach, they could drive into the village to shop, out to the fishing port at Montauk, over to Sag Harbor to catch a movie, or to sightsee along the country lanes with a picnic lunch. For the first few days they took advantage of all those options.

On Saturday, when the innkeeper, Arnold Bayley, told them about the fair in nearby Springs, and how much fun it was for the youngsters, TJ was out the door and in the car in record time. The entire six-mile drive was spent assuring him that he could see and do everything the fair had to offer. Fitz had to hold his hand to keep him from racing down Fireplace Road toward the colorful booths and lawn games packed with excited children.

At the intersection they stopped to chat with the officer directing traffic. Anxious to try his hand at the ring toss he could see in progress on the lawn, TJ tugged at his father's arm. But neither Fitz nor Nita could pass up the opportunity to spend a few moments socializing with their country colleague.

Patrolman Earl Finch greeted them with a smile, silently admiring the yellow gingham sundress that showed off Nita's figure—*Curves in all the right places*, he decided—and complemented the highlights in her lush auburn curls. At five-foot-eight she was nearly as tall as her husband, whose ginger hair their son had inherited. Together they made up what Finch described to himself as a handsome family of redheads.

"You folks from away?" he asked. "First time at the fair?"

"Yes to both questions, Officer Finch," replied Fitz, reading the name on his uniform patch. "On vacation from the city. Both my wife and I are NYPD."

Finch was naturally surprised. "You don't say? Well, we get lots of vacationing cops and firemen out this way, but I can't say I've ever met a married pair of city cops before."

Fitz made the introductions. "I'm Captain Brian Fitzgerald of the Sixth Precinct, in the West Village. My wife, Juanita, is a detective with the Two Three, up in East Harlem. And this is our boy, Timothy Juan Fitzgerald, TJ to his friends."

Finch bent down and shook TJ's hand. "Glad to know you, young fella. I hope I can call you TJ."

"Sure, sir. You can be my friend."

"That's swell, TJ. You'll have a great time at the fair," said Finch. "Us Bonackers know how to throw a party."

"What's a Bonacker?" asked the boy.

"Bonackers are the folks who come from this neck of the woods," Finch explained. "See that little crick over behind the chapel?" He gestured behind him toward a body of water just visible on the other side of the Springs Community Chapel. "That's Accabonac Crick. Anybody born within spittin' distance of that little crick is a Bonacker."

TJ was still confused. "What's a crick?"

"That's what we call a stream, like a river only much smaller. You got a big river back where you come from. That little crick is the best us Bonackers can do. It ain't much, but it suits us fine. We get clams and scallops and oysters and fish out of it, and fresh water from where it rises over there in Pussy's Pond. There's two or three springs that feed into it. That's why this neighborhood's called The Springs. That's the official name, anyhow. Folks 'round here just call it Springs."

Nita smiled down at her son. "You're getting a real

geography lesson, TJ. Something to tell your class when you get back to P.S. 40."

"You'll want to tell 'em about our local specialties, too," Finch continued. "You mustn't miss the food tent. Wait 'til you try the Bonac chowder, clam pie, and roasted corn on the cob. And save room for the peach cobbler."

"I want to try the ring toss first," said TJ, pulling his father by the hand.

Just then Finch snapped to attention. "Look out!" he shouted, and shuttled the family aside as an Oldsmobile convertible barreled up Fireplace Road, apparently oblivious to the pedestrians. The officer shook his fist at the car as it shot past.

"Hey, you, Pollock, slow down!" he called out to the driver, without apparent effect. The car continued north, then swerved into a driveway on the right, tires screeching.

"Who the heck is that?" asked Fitz.

"Crazy artist," was the reply. "Always drives like he owns the road. Even when he's sober, which ain't often. One of these days I'll yank his license."

Nita looked at Fitz. "Pollock? Not Jackson Pollock, the friend of that artist who was killed in the Village in 'forty-three?" She turned to Finch. "Fitz and I were on a case together back then—in fact that's how we met. An artist named Jackson Pollock was questioned. Turns out he wasn't involved, but I remember the name. He's pretty famous now, but in those days he was just starting out."

Finch nodded. "That's him. Around here he's famous, all right. Notorious, more like."

TJ was getting impatient. "Dad, let's go. I want to pet the goat and ride the pony."

"You two go ahead," said Nita. "I'll catch up in a minute. Just want to satisfy Officer Finch's curiosity." She had correctly perceived that her rural colleague was eager to hear the details.

TWO.

While Finch kept an eye on the road traffic, Nita filled him in.

"During the war, we had quite a number of refugee artists from Europe staying in New York," she began.

"We had some of 'em out here, too," interjected Finch. "Used to come in the summer, get out of the hot city. Liked to hang out near the beach in 'Gansett—Amagansett, that is. I think that's when Pollock and his wife first showed up."

"Well, they were in the city in October 1943, when this killing went down," Nita continued. "An artist called Wifredo Lam was found dead in his studio on West 10th Street. It looked like he was a robbery victim, and whoever killed him dressed up the body in an elaborate costume. Long story short, that wasn't what happened at all."

"What kind of costume?" Finch wanted to know.

"You ever hear of the Surrealists?" she asked. Finch

nodded, and told her they were among the wartime summer visitors.

"Then maybe you know that they play games designed to unlock the unconscious mind. At least that's the idea. Anyway, one of their games is called 'exquisite corpse.'"

Finch's brow furrowed. "You mean they kill somebody, or pretend to?"

"No, that's just what they call it. Don't ask me why. It's a drawing game, usually played by three or four people. The first person draws a head, and folds the paper over so the next person can't see it. The next person adds the next part of the body, folds it over, and so on. When it's unfolded, the figure is all mismatched parts, the weirder the better. That's the exquisite corpse."

"What's that got to do with the dead artist?"

"His body was decked out to look like one of those drawings. At first we didn't know what it meant. He was Cuban, so the detectives thought it might have something to do with Santería, the Cuban version of voodoo. I'm Cuban—at least my family's originally from Cuba—so they put me on the case to try to figure it out. But that was a phony lead. The outfit was a parody of the Surrealist game."

"What was the point o' that?" Finch asked.

"To throw the cops off in the wrong direction."

"Sounds complicated."

"It was. Fitz and I were only beat cops then, so we didn't get all the details until later, but even before they knew what the costume meant, Lam's artist friends were under suspicion. Turns out one of the wives had an affair with him back in Europe, before she got married, and when he came to New York he tried to light the flame again. They had a fight, she knocked him over, and he hit his head. It caused bleeding in his brain and killed him. It was ruled an accidental death."

"So this guy Lam and Pollock were friends in the city?"

"Yeah. Not close, but they all knew each other, went to the same parties, showed their stuff in the same art gallery. Fitz and I went to a couple of their exhibits. We didn't understand the pictures at all. Some of them were just full of funny shapes, and the ones that did have things you could recognize were all distorted. The Surrealist stuff is just plain creepy."

"You should see Pollock's paintings now," said Finch. "Look like piles of colored string all jumbled up, or yesterday's leftover spaghetti dinner. There's one hangin' in Dan Miller's general store down the road. Dan took it in trade when Pollock couldn't pay the grocery bill. He says it's an aerial view of Siberia. Might as well be, for all it means to me."

THREE.

Nita caught up to Fitz and TJ at the pony ride. This was TJ's second go-round, and he was clearly enjoying himself.

"Guess he wants to be a mounted cop," mused Fitz.

"What makes you think he wants to be a cop at all?" she countered. She saw no reason why her son should put himself in harm's way just because policing was a Fitzgerald family tradition. Especially since she had no intention of enlarging her branch of the family. As the saying goes, she had all her eggs in one basket.

They had been weaving around this issue ever since TJ was born. But Fitz was not the dictatorial type, preferring to lead by example as his own father had done, and let the boy decide for himself when the time came. He figured the chances were in his favor. After all, TJ admired his mother, too, and wasn't she on the force?

Nita decided to change the subject. "Do you remember

that exhibit we went to at Peggy Guggenheim's gallery, the one that had a Pollock painting in it? Right after we got married. She sent us an invitation to the opening—I thought it was really nice of her to remember us."

"That's where we saw all those abstract and Surrealist pictures," Fitz recalled. "More than enough for a lifetime, if you ask me. I remember the one by Matta, the guy whose wife did the number on Lam. It was full of alien-looking creatures, all having a bad day. But I don't remember a Pollock painting, do you?"

"No, but I'm sure he was in the show, because he and his wife were there—Peggy pointed them out. What was it she called him? Oh, yes, 'my new genius.' That's why I remember him. Of course there were a lot of people at the opening, so it was hard to see anything. I don't think we paid much attention, except to Matta, and then only because he was central to the Lam case. Pollock was on the sidelines then, but he got famous later on, thanks to Peggy pushing him. And that *Life* magazine article a few years ago. That really put him on the map."

"How did he wind up in this neighborhood, I wonder?" said Fitz. "Not exactly the center of the art world, is it? Kind of pretty, though, and not too remote. There's always the train, and with that Olds he could get into Manhattan pretty quick, especially at the speed he was traveling just now."

Their attention was drawn to TJ, who had reluctantly turned over the pony to the next young equestrian in line and was ready for lunch. Then the ring toss, his father promised him.

On the way to the food tent they stopped to buy a raffle ticket. The prize was a Jackson Pollock screen print, donated by the artist—a stark, black image of a strange hybrid figure struggling to free itself from that tangle of string Finch had described. Neither Fitz nor Nita cared for it, but TJ thought it was kinda interesting.

"Looks like a leapin' lizard," he declared, in the words of Little Orphan Annie, so they put down a dollar for a chance on it. The lady in the booth said they didn't have to stick around for the drawing. Somebody would call the Sea Spray if they won.

FOUR.

By mid-afternoon the Fitzgerald family had sampled all the delights the Fishermen's Fair had to offer, and were beginning to wilt in the heat. "How about a swim?" offered Nita. "Let's go back to the cottage and get changed." Located right on the beach, the inn had never bothered to install a pool. Why would anyone want to swim in chlorinated water when they had the Atlantic Ocean literally on their doorstep?

Headed to the car, they stopped to say goodbye to Officer Finch. Latecomers were having an easier time parking close to Ashawagh Hall, so his job now was keeping small children from running into the road and stopping traffic to let people cross.

"You were right about the clam pie," said Fitz, "and the peach cobbler. Can't say I was taken with the Bonac chowder, though. We're used to the red Manhattan kind, with tomatoes, or the creamy white New England style. Yours is just, well, gray."

Finch chuckled. "We don't need to disguise the clam juice. Like to see the clams swimmin' in it, make sure the cook didn't skimp."

"Last night we went to Sam's Bar and Restaurant for dinner," Nita told him. "No skimping there, and a reasonable price. The dining room at the Sea Spray is a bit steep. One of the other guests mentioned Sam's, so we drove into the village and gave it a try. We had a pizza pie with oysters on top, a first for us."

"Why don't you come back up to Springs for dinner tonight?" suggested Finch. "If you turn left up by where you're parked, down near the end of that road you'll find Jungle Pete's Restaurant."

"Jungle Pete's? Sounds exotic," said Fitz. TJ nodded enthusiastically, picturing potted palm trees, live parrots, and maybe some scary masks and stuffed animal trophies on the walls.

"Anything but," Finch replied, dashing TJ's hopes. "Pete Federico got that nickname during the war, when he served with the Marines in the Pacific. You'll like the place. Real friendly to regular folks like yourselves, good home cookin', and they have live music on Saturday nights."

With thanks for his suggestion, the family said goodbye to Finch and headed to the car. As they passed Pollock's driveway, they saw the big green Olds convertible parked beside the house.

"Wow," said TJ, impressed, "a Rocket 88. Bet it can go a lot faster than it did this morning."

"That was plenty fast enough," Nita said, with a hint of reproach in her voice. "Wonder why he was in such a rush."

"Finch seems to think that's his usual speed," replied Fitz. "No traffic lights and few stop signs on these country roads, I've noticed. Hardly any streetlights, either. Have to watch yourself with drivers like Pollock around, especially at night."

FIVE.

"He's still asleep," said Ruth Kligman as she descended the stairs to the living room in Pollock's house, where her friend Edith Metzger was waiting. The two women had changed into their bathing suits and were ready to hit the beach, but since neither of them knew how to drive, they were relying on Jackson to take them.

Edith sighed with impatience. Some weekend in the country, cooped up in a crummy old farmhouse, full of weird abstract paintings, with Ruth's drunken boyfriend. He'd already been three sheets to the wind when he'd picked them up at the train station that morning, piled them into the car, and raced back to the house like his tail was on fire. She thought he might stop at the little fair they passed, but he didn't even slow down. She and Ruth had to walk over there just to get some lunch, while he moped around the house sipping gin. He said he'd take them to the beach when they got back, but he'd gone upstairs for a nap and hadn't come back down. Now it was three o'clock and he was still dead to the world.

Ruth was full of apologies. "I'm really sorry, Edie. He's just worn-out, that's all. He'll be okay after he gets some rest. When I called to ask him if it was okay to invite you for the weekend, he was really glad to hear that you were coming."

"He has a great sense of hospitality," replied Edith sarcastically. "I guess I can catch up on my reading while he sleeps it off." She pulled a movie magazine out of her beach bag and headed for a chair on the back lawn. Ruth had told her that the creek behind the house was too shallow for swimming, and anyway the bank was all muddy. At least she could sit outside and get a little sun.

Ruth followed her into the yard. "We can go to the beach tomorrow. I'm going to call Dreesen's market and order a delivery of some steaks, vegetables, maybe an apple pie. I'll cook a nice dinner, and Jackson will be fine once he gets some food into him. I won't let him drink any more," she announced with confidence.

"He told me he wants to take us to a chamber music concert tonight," she continued. "It's in a private home, one of his rich art-collector friends is hosting it. You'll get to meet some of the interesting people he hangs around with. We'll have fun!"

Edith's idea of fun was an evening at a Midtown nightclub with friends her own age, not stuck in a gloomy country house with a bunch of stuffed shirts. They were all bound to be at least as old as Jackson. Ruth had told her that, though he looked older, he was only forty-four. To her, at twenty-five, he was ancient, almost as old as her father would have been if he had lived.

Ruth had built him up as a romantic genius, the greatest artist in America, but Edith saw only a bald, overweight, disheveled alcoholic wreck—a sorry excuse for a boyfriend. And that beard! It looked less like he'd grown it deliberately than like he couldn't be bothered to shave, or had forgotten how. Apparently he'd also forgotten that he had guests. She resigned herself to a weekend of boredom and looked forward to Sunday night's train trip home.

"Let's go over to Jackson's studio," suggested Ruth. "I want to show you more of his paintings. The brilliance, the energy, the power! Then you'll understand why I love him so deeply, so passionately," she gushed. Taking Edith by the arm, she led her across the yard to the converted barn where Jackson worked—or rather where he used to work. It had been more than a year since he had touched a paintbrush.

In the anteroom where the artist kept his tools and art storage, one wall was lined with racks full of stretched canvases dating back to the 1930s. No one wanted the figurative and semi-abstract stuff from before he started slinging paint around like a wild man, throwing it in the critics' faces, so to speak. *Jack the Dripper*, they called him. After a string of negative reviews the figures came back, but with a sinister twist. That didn't work out too well—the critics liked them, but the collectors didn't. So he started casting about for a new direction, finally returning to his earlier abstract technique, before the liquid paint pouring that got him all that notoriety. Then it all just fell apart when he dove into the bottle and couldn't climb out.

Ruth urged Edith into the studio proper. All around the room Pollock had propped up a virtual exhibition—big canvases and small ones, a couple of early works that he kept out as reference points, and a few drawings tacked to the walls. Sunshine streamed in through a big window in the north wall, bathing the whole space in natural light.

"See what I mean, Edie?" Ruth gasped with delight. "Magnificent! No one can touch him for sheer daring! All the other painters were stuck on Picasso, couldn't get past him, but Jackson just *flew right over* him!" She threw out her arms and whirled around, as if she were about to take wing herself.

How Ruth could get so excited over a bunch of meaningless paintings, nothing but overblown doodles, was beyond Edith's ken. She was used to her friend's extreme moods—either over the moon about something or down in the dumps of self-pity—but it was usually prompted by something Edith could understand, like a call from her father, a philanderer whom she glamorized, or a fight with her boss at the art gallery where she worked as a receptionist. Lately it had been all about Jackson, her devotion to him, how thrilling it was to be the lover of such a genius. That was the upside. The downside was his drinking, his mood swings, his inability to paint, her doubt that she could get him back on track.

Edith tried and failed to look enthusiastic. "I'm sorry, Ruthie," she conceded, "I just don't get it. You tell me he's a great artist, so you make allowances, and I guess you really love him or you wouldn't put up with him, but I don't see a future for you." Her own situation made her wary.

"After all," she reminded her, "he's married."

SIX.

While Nita and Fitz relaxed in canvas chairs under large umbrellas on the Sea Spray's beach, TJ was busy building a sand castle and burying his father's feet with what he excavated from the moat. Although he knew how to swim, he had strict instructions not to go in without one of his parents—this far east, the ocean was much more treacherous than at Coney Island or in the Rockaways. The water was colder out here, too, and they had been warned about rip currents, especially now during hurricane season. Even when the local weather was calm, a storm far out at sea could churn up the water along the shore. Back in the old days, they were told, when bathing suits were much bulkier, stakes with long ropes attached would be driven deep into the sand. Bathers would cling to the ropes to keep from getting dragged under.

As the afternoon wore on, they began to think about dinner.

"Let's take Officer Finch's advice and go up to Jungle Pete's," suggested Nita. "Do you think we need a reservation?"

"I'll go check," said Fitz. "There's a pay phone in the lobby." He shook the sand off his feet, threw on a robe, and headed for the inn.

He returned with the news that the restaurant didn't take reservations. In fact Nina Federico, the owner's wife, who had answered the phone, had been amused by the suggestion.

"This is Springs, honey. Just walk on in, and come as you are." He told her he was wearing a bathing suit. "Then maybe you'd better slip on a pair of long pants, and wear a shirt so you don't get the ladies all het up. Us Bonac gals are pretty hot-blooded," she teased.

"Don't worry," he assured her. "My wife will see to it I'm decent, and she can beat off any competition."

Nina's response was a hearty laugh. "This lady I gotta meet. If she likes to dance, the music starts around eight, eight thirty, depending on when the band turns up, and whether they're sober. If they are, it takes 'em a while to warm up."

Fitz returned to the beach with his report: show up any time, and wear your dancing shoes. "Sounds like fun, though I don't know how much TJ will enjoy it." He turned to his son. "What do you think, buddy?"

"It's okay, I like to watch you and Mom dance," the young diplomat replied, earning chuckles from his parents. They often took a turn or two after dinner, especially if one of the Big Bands was on the radio. Like most of his school-mates, TJ preferred rock 'n' roll, but he appreciated Benny Goodman's off-beat rhythms and exciting clarinet solos. And he enjoyed the way his folks glided around the living room in each other's arms, his dad handsome and manly like Gene Kelly and his mom as graceful as Cyd Charisse.

After thirteen years of marriage, Nita and Fitz still sparked when they embraced, and the music made it all the more romantic. Just when TJ would be thinking how goopy grownups could be, they'd beckon him to join in, and all three of them would hi-de-ho with Cab Calloway or swing and sway with Sammy Kaye.

By the time the family had washed off the sand and salt in the cottage's outdoor shower and changed their clothes, it was nearly seven, but TJ wasn't quite ready for dinner.

"Please," he asked, "can we go to the inn and watch *The Gene Autry Show?*" While exploring the Sea Spray on arrival he had spotted the television set, donated by ball-room dancing entrepreneur Arthur Murray and his wife Kathryn, in the main lounge. The Fitzgeralds had no set of their own, but some of their friends did, and Satur-day evenings often found them clustered on a neighbor's couch, soaking up the adventures of the Singing Cowboy and his horse, Champion.

"How do you know that's what other folks will want to watch?" asked Nita. "After all, there are two other networks to choose from. Maybe they'll be tuned to something else."

TJ was undeterred. "*Por favor,* please, let's just go see," he begged, and Fitz gave in. "Sure, why not take a look," he agreed. So off they went to the inn, while Nita put the finishing touches on her makeup. Not that her warm skin tones, heightened by her afternoon on the beach, needed enhancement. The sun had brought out a sprinkling of freckles on her smooth cheeks, which only added to her allure. She thought they made her look immature, so she tried to hide them with foundation, which just sat on the surface of her skin like a mask. She wiped off the makeup in disgust.

Accepting her sun-kissed condition, she contented herself with a light touch of lipstick. *I've got to wear a big hat from now on,* she decided, *or I'll never hear the end of it back at the station. They'll be calling me* las pecosas *behind my back, and maybe right to my face!*

A little after half past seven Fitz returned, with a delighted TJ in tow. They had caught *The Gene Autry Show*'s season finale, which had attracted every youngster at the Sea Spray and plenty of adults as well.

"Let's go get dinner. I could eat a horse," Fitz announced, "a big one like Champion!" Over TJ's protests, he began to describe the various cuts of horsemeat and how to cook them.

Nita interrupted before things got too grisly. "Fish is on tonight's menu—remember where we are. The local specialties are the best."

The guys concurred. "Fish it is, then. Off we go."

SEVEN.

As they pulled into the Jungle Pete's parking lot, four men were piling out of a jalopy. One carried a saxophone, and two others struggled with a double bass jammed into the backseat and a drum kit in the trunk. The fourth man, apparently the piano player, held some sheet music, a pack of cigarettes, and four bottles of beer. This wasn't their first stop of the evening.

"Looks like our timing is good," observed Fitz. "Let's get a table."

They stepped inside to find an unadorned interior, a single large room lined with knotty pine and lighted by imitation candle bulbs in shaded lamps. A mirrored bar ran the length of the wall opposite the entrance, and a small raised bandstand with an upright piano occupied one corner. A large window air conditioner struggled against the evening heat.

A lively crowd nearly filled the room, where Nina Federico met them with a genial greeting.

"You the fella who called from the Sea Spray?" she asked Fitz. "C'mon in, and welcome. This must be that tough cookie you're married to, right?" She cast an appraising eye at Nita, who blushed and asked her husband, "What have you been telling her?"

"Just that you'd protect me from the predatory females in this neighborhood," he confessed. "I told her you could handle any unwanted advances they might make."

"Sure she can," piped up TJ. "My mom's a cop!" In spite of the surrounding chatter, his voice carried far enough to cause a lull in the conversation, while men and women alike turned to take a good look at the newcomers. Nita blushed even more deeply. "Not so loud, TJ," she scolded, and advised their hostess that she was strictly off duty.

"You're okay, honey, as long as you're not armed. This bunch can get pretty rowdy, especially on a Saturday night, but we stop short of gunplay."

"I'm relieved to know that," Nita replied, "and anyway, I left my service revolver in my beach bag." She scowled at TJ, who looked appropriately sheepish. "I hope we can sit somewhere out of the limelight."

"Right over here," said Nina. "Pete's just clearing a table for you." They stepped past the crowd at the bar and headed to a somewhat quieter corner. After the first flush of curiosity had passed, the locals went back to their conversations and the band began to set up.

Pete Federico returned with menus and a boat cushion for TJ's chair.

"Tonight's special is striped bass," he announced, "just caught today. Comes with mashed potatoes and coleslaw." Turning his attention to TJ, he added, "Or we got spaghetti and meatballs if you don't like fish."

"Striped bass sounds great," Fitz told him. "That good for you, too, son?"

"Sure, Dad," said TJ. "Can I have a ginger ale?"

"And for the grownups?" asked Pete.

"My wife and I will take Knickerbocker, if you have it." Pete said he did, and promised to bring their drinks over right away. Meanwhile the piano player was warming up, the drummer was assembling his kit, and the two other musicians were at the bar ordering lubrication.

As the quartet assembled, a few taps on a glass brought relative quiet, and Pete made his announcement.

"Hey, everybody, you're in for a treat tonight. We got our own Buzzy Hand at the keyboard, Roy Conway on the bull fiddle, Russ DiGate on drums, and on sax we got a special guest artist all the way from Southampton, Larry Rivers. These boys are real versatile, so just shout out what you want to hear and they'll play it."

"Blue Moon!" came a loud voice from the bar, and the band launched into an upbeat rendition that brought several couples to the dance floor. Nita and Fitz decided to sit out until after dinner, which arrived not long after their drinks.

"Here's your fish, broiled up nice and crisp," said Pete as he placed the dishes before them. "The missus does all the cookin'. She spreads a little Hellmann's on top so it gets a tasty crust, and it keeps in the juices." He turned to Nita. "Tell me how you like it."

She took a mouthful of the plump fillet and savored it. "This is the best fish I ever tasted," she declared, obviously sincere. Fitz and TJ were nodding in agreement, and Pete's smile lit up the room.

"Finest kind," he said, using a Bonac expression of hearty approval. "Nothin' beats striped bass the way my Nina fixes it. You folks enjoy, and let me know if you want anything else."

The Fitzgeralds were not the only family in Jungle Pete's that night. By the time they had finished their meal and Nita and Fitz had taken a few turns on the dance floor, they had met other couples with children, including Nina and Pete's grandson Mike Collins, a boy about TJ's age, who offered to teach him how to fish.

"I got a rowboat tied up behind the General Store," Mike told his new friend, "and if the weather holds I'll be goin' out on the crick tomorrow after church. You're welcome to come along, I got an extra rod." Fitz gave his permission, and the date was made.

It was after ten, past TJ's bedtime, when they headed out to the car. Even after dark it was sultry, the still air heavy with humidity. Nita had no need of the sweater she'd brought in case the evening turned chilly. Fitz cast an admiring glance toward her bare shoulders, still dewy from dancing. Since she'd won promotion to detective, she no longer had to wear the unflattering policewoman's outfit that hid her shapeliness. Fitz much preferred her out of uniform. *And out of that pretty dress, too,* he said to himself, anticipating the night to come.

"What a great place," he remarked as they crossed the parking lot. "I'm sure glad Officer Finch told us about it." He opened the passenger door and pulled over the front seat so his son could climb in back. In spite of his excitement at the prospect of tomorrow's fishing trip, TJ was having a hard time keeping his eyes open. He flopped on the seat and promptly fell asleep.

Fitz looked down at his small limp body and felt a wave of emotion sweep over him. The boy was growing so fast, eager to learn, excited by every new experience, yet still so young, innocent, and vulnerable. He knew that, for TJ's sake as well as his own, he had to keep his protectiveness in check, had to encourage his son's independence and self-reliance, but it was a struggle. The love he felt for his only child sometimes overwhelmed him.

He glanced at Nita, grinned, and shook his head. She knew what he was feeling; she felt it herself. Stepping close, she put her arm around his neck and drew him to her. As they kissed, a round of applause came from the bar's porch, where a few locals were getting a breath of fresh air.

Startled, they broke apart, then laughed and waved good night as they drove off down Fort Pond Boulevard toward Fireplace Road.

EIGHT.

"Damn, this road is dark," observed Fitz. The night was clear, but with hardly any moon. "It's black as your hat out there. Once you get away from the bar's lights, there's nothing. Not even house lights, all the good Christians must be in bed. I'm glad both headlights are working, and we know where we're going."

They turned right off Fort Pond Road and headed south on Fireplace Road, passing Pollock's house and Ashawagh Hall, with no lights on at either place.

"When I mentioned to Mr. Bayley that we were driving to Springs for dinner, he told me to watch out for deer on the road after dark," said Nita. "They can do a lot of damage to a car, he said."

"Keep your eyes peeled, then," Fitz replied. "Can't be too careful, and there's no rush to get back. TJ is sound asleep."

As they passed the Gardiner Avenue intersection and

headed toward the road's major curve, they saw headlights approaching, well to their left but coming up fast. "Looks like he's not worried about hitting a deer," said Fitz.

Suddenly the oncoming car veered sharply into their lane, cut across in front of them, careened into the woods on their right, and flipped end over end.

His heart in his mouth, Fitz slammed on the brakes as Nita braced herself against the dashboard and TJ rolled off the backseat and onto the floor behind her. As they came to a stop, their lights showed the other car lying upside down among the trees, its horn blaring. It was a green convertible, an Oldsmobile Rocket 88.

"Jesus Christ," blurted Fitz. "That's Pollock's car!"

Fitz pulled off the road, and he and Nita jumped out. TJ, wide-awake now, followed them. The body of a woman lay by the roadside, and as they approached they could hear her moaning. Nita crouched down beside her, looking for apparent injuries, ready to apply first aid.

Fitz got between the women and his son, blocking his view. He was a protective father, but also a seasoned policeman who knew how to take charge of a situation. After nearly two decades on the force, he was no stranger to accident scenes. He had to raise his voice to be heard over the wrecked car's horn.

"TJ, I want you to go across the street quickly and wake up the people in that house over there. Be careful, look both ways before you cross, just like in the city. Tell the folks to call the police, and an ambulance."

Just then a light went on in the house. "That horn could wake the dead," said Fitz. "Go on now. Tell them there's at least one injured person, probably more. Get them to make those calls right away."

Stifling his curiosity, TJ did as he was told. As soon as he was safely away from the scene, Fitz turned his attention to the wreck. He assumed that the driver was Pollock, not the injured woman, whom he vaguely recognized. When the car had passed them that morning, he had glimpsed her and a companion in the backseat. As they rushed by, she'd turned to look back toward Ashawagh Hall, her dark curls billowing around a pretty young face. He thought he had seen that face again while they were having lunch at the fair.

His headlights now showed it caked with dirt and scraped along one cheek, where the woman's head had apparently hit the pavement. Nita had rolled up her sweater as a pillow, but cautioned Fitz as he knelt beside her.

"Best not to try to move her, she may have internal injuries. I've been trying to get her to talk, give me her name, but she's only semiconscious. I hope the ambulance gets here soon."

Fitz stood up. "I'd better have a look around for the driver. Hope to God he was thrown clear, too." He moved off the road and into the woods.

The Oldsmobile's headlights cut a path of visibility through the undergrowth. Fitz's first impulse was to try to silence the horn by turning off the engine, but that would also douse the lights. He decided to do it anyway, to relieve the mechanical scream that made the accident scene all the more macabre. The windshield was crushed, but the space between the door and the driver's seat allowed enough room for him to get his arm under the wheel. Groping blindly at the dashboard, he found the ignition key and turned it, killing the engine. Abruptly the woods were plunged into darkness and silence.

With the horn's echo still in his ears, Fitz returned to his own car and positioned its headlights toward the scene. They picked out a human form a few yards in front of the Olds, off to one side, sprawled at the base of an oak tree.

As Fitz approached, he detected no movement, heard no sound other than his own footsteps rustling through the leaves. He saw that it was a man—Pollock, he presumed—lying on his right side with his eyes closed and his mouth slightly open, as if he were asleep. Fitz bent down and pressed his fingertips against the neck, just under the jaw, and felt no pulse.

There was nothing more to be done, so he decided to leave any further examination to the local authorities. He returned to where Nita was standing watch over the injured woman.

"I found the driver," he told her, "he's dead. Looks like he was thrown out when the car flipped. Probably broke his neck when he hit the ground. Looks like this gal had better luck."

Just then a patrol car pulled up and out climbed Officer Finch.

"The Bennetts phoned it in," he told them. "Your boy gave them the information. I live just around the corner on Gardiner, and I got the radio call."

"What about an ambulance?" asked Nita. "This woman is injured, though I don't know how badly. She needs immediate medical attention."

"Doc Abel will be here soon. The ambulance will take a while, has to come from Southampton, but the doc will see to her."

"There's a dead man in the woods," said Fitz. "Must be Jackson Pollock. That's his car, the one you pointed out to us this morning."

"Let's go take a look," said Finch, and the two men headed past the overturned car to where the body lay. Finch pulled out a flashlight and focused it on the face. "Sure enough, that's him all right. Can't say I'm surprised. He's been asking for it for a long time."

They walked back toward the Oldsmobile. "Car's pretty well totaled," observed Finch, playing his flashlight over the wreck. Suddenly he stopped, and trained the light on the passenger side. A bare arm, nearly covered by leaves, protruded from behind the seat.

"Hold it, there's somebody in there! Looks like another woman."

While Finch held the light, Fitz dropped to his knees and felt the wrist for a pulse. Nothing. "I think she's dead, too, but I can't be sure. Should we try to get her out, or wait for the doc?"

By this time a couple more cars had pulled up, and several onlookers were standing at the roadside. "Hey, bub!" shouted Finch, "you there, Dick Talmage, come give us a hand." The burly plumber advanced toward the Olds, and Finch explained the situation. "You and me are gonna push this thing over toward the driver's side, and our friend Fitz here'll try to pull her out from under."

Talmage motioned back toward the road, and another volunteer appeared. With three men pushing, the Olds rolled over enough for Fitz to get hold of the woman under the arms and drag her free of the car. As her body emerged, covered with dirt and leaves, her head flopped back alarmingly and a pair of vacant blue eyes stared up at Fitz.

"She's done for," he told the men. "Pollock took her with him."

NINE.

When William G. Abel, M.D., finished examining the injured woman, he told Officer Finch, "We'll have to take her to Southampton Hospital in the patrol car. We've had two other auto accidents tonight, and both ambulances are out. I don't detect any broken bones, but she's badly shaken up. Might be bleeding internally, probably has a concussion. I want to get her into X-ray right away. I can stabilize her head and neck."

From his car trunk, Abel retrieved a plywood backboard and two small sandbags. Gently, he pushed the board under the victim's head and shoulders, and laid the sandbags on either side of her head. He and Finch lifted her onto the patrol car's backseat. The doctor leveled the backboard with his medical bag and slipped onto the seat beside his patient, holding her legs in his lap.

Finch took Fitz and Nita aside. "I'd be obliged if you'd wait until the coroner gets here," he said. The couple assured him they would. "You're important witnesses, and he'll be wanting to take your particulars. A formal statement can wait until tomorrow."

"Let's get moving, but not too fast, I don't want her jostled," called out Abel. "Turn on the siren." Finch did as instructed, and the car backed out onto Fireplace Road and turned toward Montauk Highway and the hospital, seventeen miles to the west.

It was a quarter past eleven when Dr. John Nugent, the Suffolk County coroner, arrived. By that time a substantial crowd had gathered, and the Fitzgeralds were eager to get their son to bed. TJ had returned just in time to see Finch's car leaving—the Bennetts had kept him safely inside with milk and cookies while traffic around the crash site was at its worst. Nita had collected him with thanks, and now had him bundled in the backseat of the Fitzgerald family car, out of sight of the corpses.

An ambulance and two more police officers had also arrived. One directed traffic, while the other helped Nugent with his examinations. Both Pollock and the unidentified female passenger were pronounced dead at the scene, and the coroner ordered the bodies removed to the funeral parlor in East Hampton village.

"I understand you saw it happen," said Nugent to Fitz, who explained that they'd been on their way back to the Sea Spray cottage when Pollock's car had cut them off and swerved into the woods. "He was going pretty fast," Fitz told him. "Looked to me like he lost control on that curve, where the concrete road ends and the blacktop begins."

Nugent jotted down the funeral parlor's address on the back of his card and handed it to Fitz. "You and the missus come to Yardley and Williams tomorrow morning, say around eleven. I can get all the details then. Sorry your boy had to see this. From what the neighbors tell me, Pollock was a menace. Too many like him on the roads out here."

Nugent was familiar with the scenario, although this particular weekend would prove to be exceptional. He would soon examine eight more fatalities from the area, all of them involving drunk driving.

TEN.

Sunday, August 12

Assuming they'd be going to mass on Sunday, Nugent had given them a late morning appointment, but the Fitzgeralds were not churchgoers. Both Nita and Fitz had lapsed long ago, and they believed it was hypocritical to send their son to services they didn't attend themselves. So they spent the morning relaxing on the cottage porch, reading the Sunday paper supplied by the inn, enjoying the sea breeze, and thanking the God they didn't worship that Pollock's car had swerved when it did.

When it was time to leave, Emily Green, the Sea Spray's housekeeper, agreed to look after TJ while his parents reported to the coroner. "But I'm a witness, too!" he protested.

"You were asleep in the backseat," said Nita.

TJ was persistent. "I saw the lady lying in the road, the one you were helping."

"She's not what they want to talk to us about," said Fitz rather sternly, dismayed at his son's morbid desire to visit the funeral parlor that doubled as the local morgue. "They want to know about the circumstances. Anyway, it's just for routine formal statements. It's boring, but necessary. We do it all the time, your mother and I, but on the receiving end."

Yardley and Williams catered to the deceased in a charming old frame house on Newtown Lane. Carolyn Williams greeted Fitz and Nita at the door, keeping her voice low. "Dr. Cooper is expecting you," she whispered as she led the way down a carpeted hall lined with upholstered seats and occasional tables laden with tasteful flower arrangements.

"The coroner, Dr. Nugent, is handling a case of multiple accident deaths in Southampton," she continued sotto voce, "so he asked Francis Cooper, one of our best local men, to fill in." Nita wondered why she spoke so softly, considering that her clients wouldn't know the difference if she shouted at the top of her lungs.

As if on cue, Mrs. Williams explained, "We have a viewing in progress, just a small family gathering in the blue chapel." The faint sound of canned organ music could be heard coming from behind a closed door on the right. *Of course*, said Nita to herself, *the living are here as well as the dead.*

A door at the end of the hallway led to a staircase that took them to the basement, where the décor was strictly utilitarian. A double outside door, opening to a ramp where ambulances and hearses could load and unload out of sight, dominated one wall of an anteroom, where a faint chemical odor hung in the air. A plain wooden desk and chair stood in a corner, next to a smaller door that led to the embalming room. A few hooks on the door held lab coats and Dr. Cooper's seersucker jacket. A bench and several chairs were ranged around the walls.

From behind the desk, Cooper rose as they entered. He was a small, rather fastidious-looking man, wearing a white shirt and bow tie. They assumed he had come straight from church to attend to this sad business at the coroner's behest. He drew a couple of chairs up to the desk, and politely asked them to sit.

"Earl Finch tells me that you're both New York City police officers," he began. "I'm glad to know that, makes my job a lot easier." He leaned toward them. "And it's going to be helpful with the investigation."

"How do you mean?" asked Fitz.

"There's a complication," said Cooper. "I autopsied the young woman this morning. She has a broken neck, sustained in the accident, but that's not what killed her. That injury occurred postmortem. She died of asphyxiation."

Nita and Fitz looked at the doctor, and then at each other, in amazement. Nita broke the silence. "You mean she was already dead when the car crashed?"

"That's right. Her fatal injuries weren't apparent until we got her cleaned up. There's bruising on both sides of her throat, and her trachea is compressed." He looked at them with a steady gaze.

"Someone strangled her."

ELEVEN.

"There's another problem," Cooper continued. "We don't know who she is. There was no identification on her. She's not a local girl, and I have no idea how she came to be in the car with Pollock and the other girl, also unidentified—she's still unconscious. Do you happen to know anything about them?"

"I thought I recognized the injured girl," said Fitz. "I think she was in the car with Pollock when he passed us on Fireplace Road yesterday morning. We were on our way to the Fishermen's Fair and stopped to talk to Officer Finch when Pollock drove by, going way too fast, and she was in the backseat. Then I saw her again later, walking around the fair. I didn't see the other girl's face, but there were two of them in the car when it went by us."

Just then the hall door opened and three people came down the stairs with Mrs. Williams. "These folks are here about the accident," she explained.

A distinguished-looking dark-haired man, casually dressed in slacks and an open-necked shirt but with an air of elegance about him, stepped forward, shook Cooper's hand, and nodded politely to the Fitzgeralds. Nita pegged him as Hispanic, but when he spoke it was with an English accent. He gave his name, a Spanish one.

"I am Alfonso Ossorio, a close friend of Jackson Pollock, as are Jim and Charlotte Brooks here." He gestured to his companions, fellow artists who had known Pollock and his wife, Lee Krasner, for years. "I hosted a private concert at my home in Georgica last night. Jackson was supposed to be there, but he never arrived." He paused, obviously distressed, then pulled himself together.

"We are here to help in any way we can. I've told Carolyn Williams that I'll be responsible for the funeral expenses."

Cooper thanked him, and introduced Nita and Fitz.

"These folks saw the accident happen. Pollock's car cut right in front of them on Fireplace Road and crashed into the woods. I was just getting ready to take their formal statements, so if you and your friends will be good enough to wait upstairs I'll be with you shortly."

"Certainly, Doctor," said Ossorio as he turned toward the stairs. "Oh, by the way, Jackson told me he'd be bringing two young ladies who were visiting him for the weekend. I understand they were with him in the car, and that one of them was also killed."

Cooper was suddenly very interested. "Do you know who they were?"

"We do," said Charlotte Brooks. "They came out to our cottage in Montauk late yesterday afternoon. Jackson was acting very strange, didn't even introduce the girls, just brought them in, sat them in the living room with me, and hustled Jim out the door, said he wanted to see his new work."

"I had to remind him that our studios were destroyed by the hurricane two years ago," said her husband, "so I had nothing out here to show him. All the paintings I've done since then are in the city. Charlotte's too. He had completely forgotten that. He seemed disoriented, sort of lost. I'm sure he'd been drinking, and I try to avoid him when he's in that condition. But he said he wanted to talk, so we sat on the beach for a while. He didn't say anything, just stared out over the water, and all of a sudden I saw tears rolling down his cheeks. I didn't know what to do, so I just sat there and waited for him to move. Eventually he got up and walked back to the cottage, piled the girls into the car and left."

"I guess he and Jim were out there for about half an hour," Charlotte said. "So I tried to make the girls feel welcome. One of them, Ruth Kligman, I'd met before. Jackson had brought her to a couple of parties." She frowned. "He was having an affair with her, and not making a secret of it. His wife, Lee, was furious. She's no doormat, believe me—not the type to look the other way. She gave him an ultimatum, she said, her or me, and Jackson was shillyshallying. What a fool, to think he could keep Ruth on the string and still have Lee to manage his life."

"What about the other girl?" asked Cooper.

"Oh, yes, sorry," said Charlotte. "I'm getting off track. Ruth introduced her as Edith Metzger, a friend from the city. She embarrassed the poor young woman by telling me that Edith was also involved with a married man— her boss at the beauty salon where she works—and didn't know how to handle it, as if I could give them advice on successfully managing adultery! I could see how uncomfortable Ruth's remarks were making her, so I changed the subject."

Cooper thanked Charlotte sincerely. "We had no identification for either of them, so you've been extremely helpful. As Mr. Ossorio mentioned, one of them was killed." He said nothing about the cause of death. "Since you met them both, would you be willing to identify the body?"

Brooks put his arm protectively around his wife's shoulders, but she had no need of moral support. She returned Cooper's gaze steadily. "Of course," she told him. "I'll be fine, Jim, don't worry."

"I know you will," he said, "but I'll go in with you. I met them both, too."

Cooper rose. "Just wait here a moment, please." He took one of the lab coats off the hook, entered the embalming room, where the autopsy had been conducted, and closed the door.

Ossorio, who had been listening intently to Charlotte and Jim, finally spoke.

"Right after Lee left, Jackson brought Ruth to our place. Paraded her around the house like a tour guide, trying to impress her, and he succeeded. Ted and I just stood back and watched. Then we saw her again at Dorothy Norman's a couple of weeks ago. She came in clinging to Jackson's arm, tarted up like a Seventh Avenue mannequin, entirely inappropriate for a country house party. Frankly, I snubbed her. I have far too much respect for Lee to make polite conversation with some little homewrecker. Mind you, I can't say Jackson was exactly solicitous to her. In fact he pretty much ignored her as well. She was painfully de trop." He grinned maliciously. "I'd like to have been a fly on the wall when they got home. I'll bet she gave him hell."

"No sooner was Lee out of the house than he moved Ruth in," said Charlotte, disgusted. "I don't think he even waited until her ship had cleared New York harbor."

In order to break their stalemate, Lee Krasner had decided to take a long-planned voyage to Europe, using the estrangement to make up her mind whether or not to divorce Jackson. Aware of her unfailing belief in his genius, as well as her frustration at his inability to work and the deep psychic wound caused by his infidelity, her friends had urged her to take the trip. *It's just an infatuation,* they told her. *It can't last. She won't be able to put up with his moods; she doesn't have your patience. Don't give up now, just let it run its course. By the time you return in the fall,* they said, *it will all be over.*

What they didn't mention was that Ruth was more than twenty years younger than Lee, attractive verging on beautiful, and blessed with a voluptuous body that she displayed to advantage, advertising her sexuality in ways that Lee no longer could. In the tiny avant-garde art world of her pre-Pollock days, Lee had been renowned for an alluring figure that compensated for a homely face, a vivacious personality and an air of self-assurance that, together with her obvious talent and commitment, made her stand out both socially and professionally.

Now, at age forty-seven, Lee had become a strident, smothering presence whose chief marital role was as her husband's nursemaid. She was also making great progress artistically, having produced a series of innovative collages that earned favorable notices when they were shown in New York City the previous fall, while Jackson had not painted at all for more than a year. Who could blame him for catching Ruth when she threw herself at him?

TWELVE.

Five months earlier

An aspiring artist who worked as an assistant to the director of the Collector's Gallery on West 56th Street, Ruth Kligman had set her cap for Pollock when she learned from a friend that he was the top dog in the vanguard pack. She had already seen his work at the nearby Sidney Janis Gallery, and was intrigued by it. *How can I meet him?* she had asked, and was told to go to the Cedar Tavern, an artists' hangout on University Place, any Tuesday night. Pollock was seeing a psychiatrist in the city on Tuesdays, driving in from Springs or taking the train, and as soon as his session was over he'd head for the bar and his drinking buddies. Often he'd stay over at the Hotel Earle, on the other side of Washington Square Park, so he could hold court at the Cedar late into the night.

Ruth was savvy enough to know that she couldn't just walk into the place and make a beeline for Pollock. For one thing, they'd assume that an unescorted woman was a hooker and she'd promptly find she had an escort, in the person of the waiter, who would accompany her to the door. For another, how would she recognize him? Her friend's vague description—middle aged, medium height, bald, bearded—probably fit a dozen or more of the Cedar's regulars. Once inside, she could ask someone, or just wait until someone either pointed him out or called him by name, but she needed a date to get her in.

As luck would have it, one of her gallery's artists, a young hopeful named George, was dithering over whether or not to go ahead with a one-man show of his new work, wholeheartedly in favor one minute and the next minute sure he wasn't ready for a solo outing. He needed to talk it over face-to-face, he told her on the phone, and suggested meeting at his local watering hole, which happened to be the Cedar, for a drink and reassurance.

"Of course," she said, thrilled by the coincidence. "How about next Tuesday night?"

"Make it ten p.m.," he replied, and the date was set.

Determined to take full advantage of this opportunity, Ruth dressed to impress. Wearing an eye-catching white coat over a form-fitting black dress, shod in spike heels that flattered her legs, with her hair expertly styled in an updo by Edith that afternoon, she crossed the threshold of the Cedar Tavern determined to seduce the most important painter in New York. The appointment with her indecisive artist was simply a fortunate convenience, to be concluded as quickly as possible.

But as soon as she got inside, she realized that she was overdressed and out of her depth. This was no cocktail lounge, with soft lighting and piano music. It was a noisy, smoky, no-frills saloon populated by serious boozers lining the long bar and filling the battle-scarred tables and shabby booths. Almost all of them were men, wearing paint-stained work clothes and arguing at top volume. A couple of boisterous female artists, just as carelessly dressed, were keeping up with them, trading wisecracks and matching them drink for drink. The few other women, apparently wives or girlfriends, either tried to carry on conversations among themselves or just sat patiently while the guys bantered on.

Ruth surveyed the room with dismay. *What a dive*, she said to herself. *I don't think this is going to work. Maybe I can arrange to be at Janis when he comes in, it's only a block from where I work. He must have to meet with his dealer once in a while to discuss business. I can call David, Sidney's assistant, and find out when he's expected. I could break the ice by telling him how much I admire his paintings. And I wouldn't have to shout at him to be heard.*

Just as she was deciding that Pollock's gallery would be a more conducive place to bump into him accidentally on purpose, George spotted her and motioned her to his booth.

"Over here, Ruth," he called, waving her on. Reluctantly, knowing she was attracting attention both as a stranger and an obvious misfit, she hurried past the ogling crowd and ducked into the booth as quickly as possible. As she passed the bar one of the female artists snickered, leaned over, and said something in the ear of her male companion, and the two had a good laugh at Ruth's expense.

Furious, she turned on the hapless George. "How could you bring me here without telling me what to expect?" she demanded.

He was taken aback. "You mean you've never been here before? I thought you knew the scene, working in an art gallery. This is where all the artists hang out."

With her naïveté staring her in the face, Ruth tried to cover her tracks. "I always visit artists in their studios, where I can look at their work and discuss it in peace. That's what I did when we picked the things for your show, remember? We can't have a decent conversation in this madhouse."

"Please don't be angry, Ruth. I just had to get out of the studio, be around other people. And I really need your advice about the show. Let me buy you a drink." She asked for a scotch and soda, and he signaled the waiter.

Taking his wave as an invitation, a couple of his friends slid into the booth.

"Got a new girl, Georgie? She's a hot number. Aren't you going to introduce us? What's your name, honey?" one of them shouted. "Hey, I could go for you," the other one chimed in. "Why don't you dump that loser and sit over here next to me?"

"Excuse me, gentlemen," said Ruth with sarcastic emphasis, "I have to powder my nose." She stood and turned to George. "If you want my advice, you'll be alone in this booth when I get back."

Making her way to the restroom, she approached a round table that seemed unusually crowded. Extra seats had been squeezed in, and a gaggle of eavesdroppers, drinks in hand, stood by attentively, hanging on every word they could pick up over the general hubbub. As she passed, she heard a bellowing voice.

"You're a fucking whore!"

Shocked and embarrassed, she turned to see an equally startled man, in a rumpled shirt under a tweed jacket, staring at her. "Oh, shit," he said, then shook his head and half rose. "That is, I'm sorry. Please, I didn't mean you. Really, it was a mistake."

He stumbled to his feet and, extending a large, nicotine-stained hand, indicated his vacant chair. "Sit down, please, and let me explain."

Without being asked, the man sitting next to him stood up and offered his chair. "Here, Jack, take my seat."

Jack. Short for Jackson? Could it be Pollock? About five foot ten, looking to be in his fifties, heavyset, scruffy beard, a fringe of hair around a bald pate—yes, it could be him.

He was watching her intently, making her uncomfortable with his scrutiny. He took both her hands in his. "You're so lovely," he said. "I can't forgive myself for offending you like that." She started to demur, but he interrupted. "Who are you? What are you involved with?"

Aware that all eyes were on them, conscious of her own rapid heartbeat, she tried to regain her composure. "I'm Ruth," she told him. "Who are you?"

"I'm Jackson."

THIRTEEN.

Sunday, August 12

Before he admitted Jim and Charlotte to the embalming room, Cooper positioned a screen in front of the gurney that held Pollock's draped body, which he had yet to autopsy. No need to subject the artist's old friends to the sight of his corpse, even under wraps. Once the screen was in place, Cooper carefully arranged the sheet that covered the woman's body, tucking it under her chin and behind her head so that only the face was visible and the marks on her neck were hidden.

He returned to the anteroom, took his jacket off the hook, and offered it to Charlotte, who was wearing only a light summer blouse, dungarees, and sneakers.

"Here, you'll need this. It's cold in there," he told her. Jim helped her slip it on and replaced his arm around her shoulders as they both prepared themselves mentally for the viewing.

Cooper opened the door. "This way, please," he said, and ushered them in.

No sooner had they entered the room than Charlotte spoke.

"It's Edith." Even from ten feet away, she was certain.

"How can you tell?" asked Nugent.

"Her hair. Both she and Ruth have dark brown hair, but Ruth's is long and wavy. Edith's hair is short, as you see, what they call a pixie cut.

"Does she have blue eyes?" Charlotte asked. Cooper said yes. "Then it's Edith for sure. I remarked on how lovely they were when I was trying to get Ruth off the subject of affairs with married men. Her eyes are brown."

Cooper thanked her, and followed the couple out to where Ossorio and the Fitzgeralds were waiting. Charlotte returned the doctor's jacket and told the others that she had identified the woman in the next room.

"We need to inform the next of kin," said Cooper. "I'll call the hospital and find out if the other woman—you say it's Kligman—is conscious. Maybe she can tell us how to get in touch with Metzger's family." He reached for the telephone, then paused.

"Has anyone been in touch with Pollock's wife? Where is she?"

Ossorio answered, "She's in Paris, at the apartment of Paul Jenkins, an artist friend, and his wife, Esther. They invited her to stay with them, so she checked out of her hotel and moved over to their place on Friday. Not realizing she would actually be there, I thought Paul would know how to reach her, so I put a call through to him early this morning.

"It was nine a.m. their time, and Lee was in the apartment. I don't know how, but she knew the call was bad news even before Paul told her. As I was explaining what happened, I heard her scream—the look on Paul's face must have given it away. He told Esther to grab her, apparently she ran to the window and he was afraid she'd do something foolish.

"He called me back later. It took an hour to calm her down, then he and Esther took charge. They canceled her return passage on the *Queen Elizabeth* and arranged a flight back to New York. I'm driving to Idlewild to pick her up tomorrow morning."

"Has he any other family who need to be notified?"

Jim spoke up. "Yes, there's his mother and four brothers. Jack was the youngest. I'm close to his brother Sanford, he's called Sande for short, knew him before I met Jack. We worked together on a big WPA mural at LaGuardia Airport in the late 'thirties. He and Jack lived together on East Eighth Street in the Village. Then Sande got married to his sweetheart Arloie, had a kid, and the WPA was winding down so he decided to give up being a painter and earn a steady living. He moved the family up to Connecticut and opened a printing shop, did some war work and commercial stuff. When their mom got too old to live alone, Sande and 'Loie took her in.

"When Sande left—spring of 'forty-two, I think it was—Lee moved in. She and Jack had both been on the WPA, getting a regular paycheck for their work as artists.

Seems like a million years ago that we had that kind of government support. But by then it was no longer a case of just doing your own paintings. After Pearl Harbor the WPA became a war services program, and they had to do propaganda posters and window displays for civil defense, things like that. But it paid the rent, and they could still do their own work after hours. By that time I'd been drafted, and I shipped out overseas, still working for Uncle Sam as an artist, but now on the army's payroll.

"After I came back stateside I was looking for a place, and Jack and Lee were thinking of moving to the country. You may remember how bad the housing shortage was then—you couldn't find an apartment in New York for love nor money. Jack told me that one of his other brothers, Jay, was taking over the Eighth Street place, but that he might rent us the front half, where Jack had his studio and a bedroom. Jay agreed, so we moved in when Jack and Lee left."

He smiled and gave Charlotte a little hug. "We weren't married then, but we got hitched a year or so later. In 'forty-eight I got a teaching job at Pratt, and we found our own apartment and bought the Montauk cottage for summers. Jack was sober then, and I really enjoyed being around him. He loved to go beachcombing, or we'd go out in the rowboat with a picnic lunch and pretend to fish. But I especially liked our studio visits. He really understood what I was driving at, and his comments were always right on target. When I went to his studio, I could feel the energy, almost like an electric charge, that went into his paintings. Lee once called it a living force, and I think that about sums it up."

Jim took a deep breath. "Where was I going with this? Off on a tangent, I'm afraid. Oh, yes, I was talking about Jack's family. Well, like I said, Sande, 'Loie and mother Stella are up in Deep River. Jay and Alma are still on Eighth Street, I think, and Charles, the eldest, is teaching out in the Midwest. Frank, the middle brother, lives near San Francisco. I'll call Sande, he'll notify the others."

He paused, and shook his head ruefully. "Stella's going to take this hard. He was her youngest, her baby boy. She always encouraged him, praised him, never scolded or criticized. She glossed over his emotional problems, just acted like they didn't exist. And she was so proud of his success."

"It'll be very hard on Sande, too," added Charlotte. "Of all the brothers he was closest to Jackson, they were only three years apart. But more than that, he was Jackson's soul mate, the shoulder he cried on before Lee came along. They lived through hard times together, and that forged a bond time and distance couldn't break. He was so disappointed when Jackson fell off the wagon, really angry with him. Not that Sande is a teetotaler, but he knew how badly alcohol affected Jackson, much worse than most people. He had no tolerance, couldn't hold his liquor at all."

FOURTEEN.

Cooper apologized to Nita and Fitz, who had been patiently waiting to give their statements, for keeping them so long, and for the diversion.

"No apology necessary," said Fitz. "The IDs are more important, and all this background is interesting. East Eighth Street is just outside my precinct—the border is Sixth Avenue—so I know the neighborhood well. Nita and I had our first date at the Cedar Tavern, when it was on West Eighth Street."

Nita poked her husband in the ribs. "It was supposed to be a business meeting, so I could report a development in the homicide case we were both working on at the time. I could have given him the information over the phone, but he insisted we meet in person."

"You've got a lousy memory," he replied with a grin. "You were the one who suggested the meeting. I just named the place." His arm went through hers. "We got the business part over with pretty quick. From then on it was pure pleasure, for me anyway."

She returned his smile. "The feeling was mutual. And still is. But please, Dr. Cooper, make your call. We can wait a bit longer. The housekeeper at the Sea Spray is looking after our son 'til we get back, but I don't want to take advantage of her. And we made a date for him to go fishing up in Springs this afternoon."

"I'll take Jim and Charlotte to my place," said Ossorio, "and we can call Sande from there. There are others to be notified as well, people in the city who may not have heard." He turned to Cooper. "When will you release Jackson's body? I'd like to be able to tell them when the funeral will be."

"I'll do the autopsy this afternoon. It should be routine, the cause of death is pretty evident. You say his wife will be back tomorrow? See if Fred can schedule the funeral for Wednesday. That should give folks enough time to make travel arrangements."

Ossorio thanked him, and left with Jim and Charlotte.

"Interesting fellow, that Ossorio," remarked Nita. "He looks Spanish, sounds English, yet he doesn't seem to be exactly either."

"I've never met him before," said Cooper, "but I've heard a lot about him. He's Filipino—Spanish father, Chinese blood on his mother's side. He bought a big estate out here a few years ago. His family's very rich, the father owns a sugar mill. He went to boarding school in England, that's where the accent comes from. But he's something of a black sheep, turned up his nose at the family business to be an artist. And he's a pansy, got a ballet dancer for a boyfriend, so I'm told. But let me get you out of here before your whole day is shot." He motioned them back to their chairs by the desk.

With a policeman's precision, as if he were reading from notes, Fitz described the accident and its aftermath, his finding Pollock's body, and Officer Finch's discovery of Metzger's body under the car. Nita gave an equally concise report of tending to Kligman, and of Dr. Abel's ministrations.

"I couldn't tell right away if Pollock was dead," said Fitz, "he looked like he might just be unconscious. He was lying on his side, so any visible injuries must have been on the side that was hidden. I didn't want to move him, but I checked the carotid, and there was no pulse."

"The cranial and thoracic lacerations are on his right side," said Cooper. "He's still in rigor, but I can feel a severe skull fracture and broken ribs."

"Officer Finch must have told you how we got the dead girl out from under the car," Fitz continued. "I didn't think there was much chance of her being alive, and when I pulled her out I could tell her neck was broken. Of course I thought that was what killed her. It was pretty dark, and she was covered in dirt and leaves, but I should have noticed the neck bruises."

Cooper hastened to reassure him. "I didn't see them

myself at first. She also has bruising on her upper arms that could easily be mistaken for dirt smudges. Of course, under the circumstances, you would assume she died as a result of the crash. If she hadn't already been dead, the broken neck certainly would have been fatal.

"I hope the Kligman girl can shed some light on this," he continued. "I'd better ring the hospital and see how she's doing. Do you mind waiting just a few minutes more while I make the call?"

Of course not, they said, and Cooper lifted the receiver and dialed a number he knew well.

"Not good," he told them, replacing the receiver. "No broken bones, but she's still not conscious. She's in severe shock, and they're afraid she's going to lapse into a coma. We need to locate her family. Metzger's, too."

FIFTEEN.

They were back at the Sea Spray a little after noontime. Nita and Fitz relieved Mrs. Green of their son and used the pay phone to call the Collins house in Springs.

"Is young Mike still interested in giving our TJ a fishing lesson?" asked Fitz. "Yes? Well, that's fine. I'll bring him right over. Sure, we can meet Mike at the General Store in about fifteen minutes."

TJ had been ready to go for the past hour, so there was no delay heading out. It was a straight run up Ocean Avenue to Main Street, a left fork onto North Main just before the windmill, under the tracks to the right fork and onto Fireplace Road.

As they came to the end of the concrete pavement, with its rhythmic thump-thump, and gained the smooth black-top, the road curved to the left. Without really thinking about it, Fitz slowed the car, then realized where he was.

On the right shoulder, a deep groove of chewed-up dirt

marked the spot where Pollock's tires had dug in, then swerved back onto the road surface. From there, skid marks ran for a couple hundred feet and ended at the woods on the left. The convertible had been towed away, and the victims' shoes and other effects had been collected, so there was little evidence of what had happened there the night before. Only a few broken branches, a couple of crushed saplings, and a freshly disturbed patch of undergrowth.

TJ, who was sitting between his parents on the front seat, craned his neck to try and look out Fitz's window, but Nita put her arm around his shoulder and drew him back.

"Nothing to see there now," she said softly. Fitz put his foot down and the car picked up speed. They reached the General Store with time to spare.

Mike was waiting on the porch, his fishing gear resting against the old church pew that served as a bench. A few well-weathered lawn chairs and a castoff picnic table were also there for the convenience of the morning kaffeeklatsch, lunchtime gossip fest, and afternoon political discussion group that gathered there daily, rain or shine. Today the weather was bright and calm, the humid air blanketing the little hamlet like damp silk.

"Howdy," said Mike, shaking TJ's hand rather formally. He was taking his instructor's role seriously. "You set here. Be right back." He ducked into the store and emerged a few minutes later with two sandwiches wrapped in wax paper, two bottles of root beer, and a small pail of wriggling worms. TJ eyed them dubiously.

"Let's go. Fish won't wait." Mike handed the bait to TJ, silently enjoying his new friend's squeamishness. Mike collected the tackle and marched his student into the side yard, where a couple of rowboats were tied up alongside a makeshift landing. TJ turned and waved to his parents as Mike launched one of the boats and they shoved off into Accabonac Creek.

"Man of few words, young Mike," observed Fitz.

"Typical Bonacker," said a voice behind him, "just like his old man, and his old man's old man." Fitz turned to find that the store's proprietor, Dan Miller, had joined them. "Besides, he's kinda upset about Jackson. They were pals. When Jackson had the Model A, he used to take Mike for rides in the rumble seat. He got on better with kids than with grown-ups. Nothin' but an overgrown kid himself.

"They'll be gone a while," Miller told them. "You folks want t'set a spell? Just made a fresh pot o' coffee." His pronunciation carried a reminder of the New England ancestors from whom he and his fellow Bonackers had descended.

"Thanks, but I'd rather have a cold bottle of pop," said Nita, fanning herself with her sun hat, and Fitz agreed.

"How about some lunch?" he suggested. "Got any more of those sandwiches?"

"You bet," replied Miller. "Got ham—that's what I gave

the boys—or homemade chicken salad today. Got some coleslaw, too." They ordered one of each sandwich, with coleslaw on the side, and two bottles of Hires root beer. "I'll have un with you," said Miller.

"Let me pay for everything," offered Fitz, but Miller said no. "The boys' lunches, and the bait, are on the Collins family tab. Your son is their guest, you wouldn't want to shame 'em. Bonackers are a prideful lot. But you can buy me a Hires if you like." He winked at Fitz. "I ain't proud."

Settled in the porch shade, food and drinks in hand, the trio surveyed all of downtown Springs in one wide glance. To the right, across the bridge that spanned the creek, was the Presbyterian chapel, with its small graveyard out back. To the left of it, on the other side of Accabonac Road, was Ashawagh Hall, the former Springs schoolhouse, now used for meetings, art shows, and all manner of community events like the Fishermen's Fair. The only amenities not visible were the Parsons blacksmith shop, north on Fireplace Road, and the "new" Springs School, vintage 1909, hidden behind Clarence King's house up ahead on School Street. From where they sat, if there hadn't been buildings in the way, a strong pitcher could have hit either one with a rock.

After satisfying his curiosity about their identities, Miller asked Nita and Fitz if they were the folks who witnessed the accident the night before. They confirmed it.

Miller shook his head. "I hate t'say it, 'cause he was a

friend o' mine, but Jackson had it comin'. He was reck-less, that's all. Bound to happen sooner or later. Shame about those young ladies, though. One dead, and the other may not make it. No excuse for that. None at all."

The couple exchanged glances. Apparently the news that one woman had been killed before the crash had not yet leaked out.

"Some folks 'round here didn't take to Jackson, but we got along fine," Miller continued. "He was a country boy at heart, grew up on farms out West, though he'd lived in New York since he was eighteen. That's where all the artists are, the galleries, the collectors, so that's where he had t'be, but after a while it started to wear him down. He told me more'n once that when he came to Springs he didn't move *to* the country, he moved *away from* the city. He said the pace was killin' him." He paused, realizing the irony of his last remark.

"He shoulda kept the Model A. That old rattletrap couldn't go more'n thirty downhill. And we got no hills in Springs."

Just then a battered pickup truck pulled up and a man in a work shirt and overalls got out. It was Mike's father, Tom Collins. Miller greeted him with the usual Bonac salute, "Howdy, bub," and got the same in return.

"Guess you know who these folks are," said Miller, nodding at the Fitzgeralds. "Your Mike is out fishin' with their boy."

"Met 'em last night," replied Collins. "Glad t'see you.

And I got a message for you. Seems you won the raffle yesterday. My sister-in-law was in charge o' the drawin'. She was gonna call the Sea Spray, but I told her you'd be up to Dan's so I'd let you know m'self."

"That's the longest speech I heard outta you in decades, Tom," teased Miller. "Congratulations, folks. What's the prize?"

Collins reached into the truck's cab, picked up a cardboard tube from the passenger seat, and handed it to Fitz.

"The Pollock picture," he said. "Now ain't that somethin'? You seein' him die and all."

SIXTEEN.

An East Hampton Town patrol car pulled in next to Collins' truck.

"What say, Earl?" asked Collins as Officer Finch emerged.

"Howdy, Tom, Dan," he replied. "I'm lookin' for the Fitzgeralds, and I found 'em." He turned to Nita and Fitz. "Doc Cooper told me you'd probably be up here. I got some news about the accident."

Fitz hoped he wasn't going to spill the beans about Metzger, though maybe he didn't know the details.

"What's cookin'?"

"Doc found Pollock's house key in his trouser pocket. I called Riverhead this morning, got a search warrant to enter the premises. I hope I can find some identification for the women. Thought it might be a good idea to take Detective Diaz along. Would that be okay, ma'am?"

"Nita, please," she advised, though she was delighted

that he had addressed her by her official title. Working out of her precinct in Spanish Harlem, she had decided to keep her maiden name so the neighborhood folks would know she was one of them and not some Irish interloper from downtown.

"I'll be glad to go with you," she told Finch. "Fitz can wait here for the boys."

Collins settled in next to Fitz, eager to hear a firsthand account of last night's tragedy.

"How fast yuh reckon he was goin'?"

"I can't say for sure, but I'd guess at least fifty, maybe sixty. His lights came up on me pretty quick. I don't mind telling you, I thought he was gonna hit us for sure, but he veered off into the woods just in time—for us, that is. Not for him, of course, or his passengers."

Collins nodded. "I hear the doc's slicin' him up now. Bet he'll find more alcohol'n blood in his veins."

Fitz marveled at the speed of the Bonac telegraph system.

"'Course he had no business foolin' round with that young gal," Collins continued. "Drivin' his wife crazy. What that poor woman put up with, even 'fore he started cheatin'. Mind you, she's a tough one—don't take t'her m'self—but I got sympathy. She'll be back t'morrow, I'm told."

Amazing, thought Fitz. *There must be few secrets around here. I'd better be extra careful not to let anything slip.*

A couple of lunch customers arrived, so Miller excused

himself and stepped inside the store. Fitz said he was comfortable where he was, and turned to watch his wife and Finch depart in the patrol car.

When they pulled into the Pollock house driveway at 830 Fireplace Road, only a few hundred feet north of the General Store, there was already another car parked by the garage. Nita got out and headed to the front of the house, but Finch stopped her.

"This way," he said, pointing to the back porch. "House has no front door. They closed it off when they put in the plumbing a few years ago. Dick Talmage told me that in addition to the full bath upstairs Lee wanted a toilet downstairs, and the only place they could fit it in was the front hall."

Nita was surprised. "You mean the house had no bathroom when they moved in?"

"That's right. Had to use a hand pump in the kitchen sink for water, and a backhouse for the call of nature. Coal stoves for heat, cookin' too. That's real country livin'."

Nita was trying to imagine how she would manage with no running water, steam radiators, gas stove or flush toilet. Not well at all, she was certain. Especially after TJ came along. But apparently there were no children to complicate the Pollocks' life, a blessing under the circumstances.

She and Finch walked to the rear of the building and

mounted the small porch that led to the back door. No need for the key, since it was already open.

"Hello? Mrs. Pollock?" called Finch. He hadn't expected to find anyone home, least of all the wife, who was supposed to be overseas, but maybe she'd smelled a rat and come back early.

Silently, he began to speculate. Maybe Ossorio was just covering for her. He could have tipped her off about the girlfriend. What if she'd shown up on Saturday night, caught her husband with the women, got into a fight, and did one of them in? An enraged wife would likely have enough strength to strangle someone she thought was her husband's lover. She certainly had the motive.

The back door opened into the kitchen. Surprisingly, instead of the small rooms one would expect in an old farmhouse, the whole ground floor had been opened up to create a single space. The wall that had once separated the kitchen from the back parlor had been demolished, and the double doors to the front parlor were removed. They could see right through the house to a pair of French doors that led to the front porch. The shades were drawn to keep out curious eyes.

Moving into the back parlor, now a spacious living and dining area, they found the stark white walls covered with Pollock's colorful abstract paintings. On the north wall behind the dining table, a huge canvas, nearly twelve feet wide, dominated the room. On the left side, a jumble of black lines reminded Nita of the print they had won in the raffle—suggestions of a figure, but scrambled and indistinct. On the right, a baleful face, blotched in blue and orange and fragmented like a patchwork quilt, stared out at them accusingly. *How dare you invade my home*, it seemed to say.

They heard footsteps on the stairs, and a tall woman in her late twenties, wearing a T-shirt, paint-flecked jeans, and a kerchief around her head, came down to meet them.

"Hello, there," she said, apparently unconcerned to find a uniformed police officer and a strange woman in the house. She must have been expecting the law to turn up at some point, possibly with a relative of one of the girls in tow.

"Who are you?" asked Finch.

She introduced herself as Cile Downs, another of the many artists who had moved to the neighborhood at Jackson and Lee's urging, bought up rundown farmhouses and converted the outbuildings into studios, turning Springs into Greenwich Village East. Some of the locals complained that they were displacing the old families, but others thought they fit right in with the community's indigenous oddballs, of whom there were plenty.

"I live up the road," she told Finch. "Charlotte called to tell me that Lee is expected back tomorrow."

"How did you get in?" he wanted to know.

"I got the key from the next-door neighbors. Lee asked them to keep an eye on the place while she was away.

Obviously she couldn't trust Jackson on his own. Of course she had no idea he wasn't actually living alone."

"What do you mean?"

"Ruth moved in the day Lee moved out. That's why I'm here, to get rid of the evidence." She corrected herself hastily. "Oh, I didn't mean that the way it sounded. Not that there was a crime or anything."

Nita glanced at Finch, who nodded almost imperceptibly. So he did know that Edith had met with foul play.

"I meant I didn't want Lee to see Ruth's clothes hanging in her closet, Ruth's makeup in her bathroom, and Edith's things are here, too. How would that look? Lee has enough to face without that." It was clear she was aware that two attractive young women were in residence, and was determined to do her best to lessen Lee's inevitable humiliation.

Nita understood perfectly. She identified herself and explained their mission. "Of course, you're right. But let us have a look around first, then you can tidy up. We won't be long. We're looking for Kligman's and Metzger's addresses."

"There's a handbag on the dining table," said Cile, pointing to a purse lying next to a white scarf. Finch thanked her and began to search it, while the two women went upstairs.

Cile had a suitcase open on the guest room's unmade bed and was filling it with women's clothing.

"All these clothes are Ruth's," said Cile, indicating the

heap of garments on the bed. "Lee wouldn't be caught dead in this vulgar stuff. She has a real sense of style, used to model for a fashion illustrator when she was younger. Still has a great figure."

"Did you find any purse or wallet?" Nita asked.

"I haven't gone through the drawers yet, just the closet." Cile pulled open the top drawer of the bureau.

"Holy cow," she exclaimed, "here's her diaphragm." She extracted a black plastic box, circular in shape, like a compact but larger and thicker. She popped it open. It was empty.

Cile snickered. "She must be wearing it. What an optimist. Jackson was way too far gone to be any use in the sack."

The women exchanged knowing looks, but Nita needed to move on. "Let's see if there's anything in there that's actually useful." She pushed aside some underwear, handkerchiefs, and a tube of spermicidal cream, and came up with a red leather wallet. Inside, behind a clear plastic window, was a return request card with Ruth's name and address.

"Now that's interesting," Nita remarked, "she lives on West 13th Street, right in my husband's jurisdiction. He's a captain at the Sixth Precinct, just a few blocks south, on Charles Street. Where are Metzger's things?"

"He put her in the master bedroom," said Cile. "She was going to use one of the twin beds. Lee and Jackson slept in separate beds." She imparted that information without further comment, but it was apparent that Jackson had chosen to share the guest room with Ruth because it had a double bed.

Cile led Nita into the sunny master bedroom on the right. The detective's experienced eye scanned the room, looking for signs of a struggle. There were none. Edith's overnight bag, still partly packed, lay on the bed nearest the door. The bathing suit that had never gotten wet was tossed on a chair, and a single sundress hung in the closet.

A makeup case sat next to the portable vanity on a shelf by the window. Cile was about to scoop it up when Nita stopped her. "Let me look around first, then you can clear up in here. It won't take me long." Compared to Ruth's elaborate wardrobe, Edith had brought much less clothing and fewer accessories. Unfortunately neither the suitcase nor the bureau contained any identification.

She thanked Cile for her cooperation, took Ruth's wallet and descended to the dining room, where Finch had finished with the handbag.

"Looks like this belongs to Metzger," he told Nita, "or rather it did." He had spread the contents out on the table. "There's a coin purse with eighty-nine cents in change, a hankie, a comb, lipstick, a compact, and a wallet with thirty-six dollars in it—probably cashed her paycheck on Friday—a return Long Island Rail Road ticket to Penn Station, and an ID card. She lived at 249 West 13th Street."

"That's the same as Kligman's address," said Nita. "I bet they were roommates."

"You're probably right," said Finch. "Kligman can confirm that when she comes to. *If* she comes to, that is."

SEVENTEEN.

As Finch's patrol car came to a stop in the General Store's parking lot, he clicked on his radio to report in. "Finch here," he told the dispatcher.

"Where are you?"

"At Dan Miller's store in Springs. I got the IDs for the two women. I'll bring 'em in now."

He shook Nita's hand. "I'm real grateful you came along. I think the Downs woman was more cooperative with you than she woulda been with me."

"Well, there was some intimate stuff she wouldn't have wanted to share with you, though I don't think it has any bearing on the case. It's too bad she got there before we did. I would have liked more time to go through the house undisturbed. There may be something we missed by not wanting to tip her about a possible homicide."

"I had a good look around downstairs while you were upstairs," he said. "No sign of a scuffle, everything in place. Dirty dishes in the sink from dinner—Doc said Metzger had eaten not long before she died."

"I didn't notice anything out of place upstairs. But Cile might have unknowingly tampered with evidence. Can't help that now. Let's hope Kligman comes to and sheds some light."

Finch headed out, and Nita was about to return to her seat beside Fitz when he rose and came out to the parking lot to meet her. "Let's walk over to the landing," he suggested. "Maybe we can see the boys from there." His real motive was to get out of earshot of the customers lounging on the porch. Several more locals who had shown up in Nita's absence were now feasting on Dan Miller's sandwiches and their daily ration of gossip. No need to add any more tasty morsels.

They strolled into the yard, and Nita filled him in on the discoveries at the house, including the fact that there was no apparent evidence of foul play.

"Both women lived at the same address," she said. "I'm guessing they shared an apartment, or knew each other from the building. But here's an interesting coincidence—their address is on your patch, West Thirteenth, number 249."

"Well, son of a gun. Can't say I recognized either of them from the neighborhood, but that would be unlikely unless they showed up at the station. When I was on the beat I used to know all the shopkeepers by name, and many of their customers as well, at least by sight. Sometimes I miss that, feel like I'm out of touch."

"Maybe they're new in the area," said Nita reassuringly. As a detective she had far more frequent contact with the residents in her precinct, while Captain Fitzgerald was often tied to his desk by administrative duties.

The sight of a rowboat, drifting toward them with oars shipped, interrupted their talk. Although hardly an expert on inland waterways, Fitz knew enough to expect a river to run downstream from its source, but the creek was flowing toward Pussy's Pond, bringing the little boat and its two young passengers effortlessly back toward the landing.

As they neared the shore, Mike locked the starboard oar and expertly maneuvered into position for Fitz to grab the bow and pull them onto the small ramp. Both boys were grinning from ear to ear, and it was easy to see why. In the bottom of the boat were a dozen blowfish, flopping about and working their rubbery mouths.

"*Papá, Mamá, ver este*, watch!" cried TJ. He picked up one of the fish by the tail and poked its belly. The creature gulped air and inflated its stomach, turning into a round ball. TJ squealed with laughter, both at the fish's uncanny transformation and at his parents' astonished expressions.

Mike, who had seen this performance many times before, focused on the practical. "Ugly, but good eatin'. Only the tail end, mind. Nothin' in the body. See?" He tapped the air sac to emphasize his point.

He hopped out of the boat, retrieved a bucket from

behind the store, and handed it to TJ. "Fill 'er up while I get the gear," he ordered.

"How many of those did you catch?" Nita asked her son as he scooped the haul into the bucket.

"Four," he answered honestly. As a neophyte fisherman, he had not yet learned to exaggerate. "Mike showed me the trick. You just stick the hook through a worm, jiggle it in the water, and they go right for it. You have to be careful gettin' the hook out, though. They've got sharp teeth. Spines on the back, too. It's best to put a rag around them while you hold them," he informed his parents with authority.

"TJ learns fast," said Mike with pride. "Finest kind." He shook his student's hand. "You keep the catch. Mr. Miller'll wrap 'em for ya."

Nita was quick to decline the offer. "Oh, no, Mike, you take them. I wouldn't know how to cook them, but I bet your mom does."

"Sure does," he replied, "knows how to clean 'em, too, but she sure don't like to. They got skin like sandpaper. Hasta wear gloves or she'll scratch up her hands." That news made Nita even more relieved that she'd turned him down.

Fitz offered to run Mike home, but the boy said he'd walk, it was only down the road. As they thanked him for his kindness to TJ, Fitz couldn't let him go without satisfying his curiosity about the creek.

"She's tidal," Mike explained. "Connected to Gardiner's

Bay. Runs back'rds twice a day. Good timin' for us, we got a free ride in."

"Speaking of which," said Fitz as they waved goodbye to Mike, "we'd better ride on back to the cottage and get TJ cleaned up. We may not be taking the fish with us, but we're sure taking their smell."

EIGHTEEN.

On the way back to the Sea Spray, Nita told TJ what was in the cardboard tube. "Yes, you won the Pollock picture," she said. "Under the circumstances, I hope you don't regret taking a chance on it."

"Oh, no!" he replied with gusto. "It's sorta creepy that he's dead, but the picture is sorta creepy, too."

Once again Fitz was dismayed at his son's ghoulish streak. *Was I like that at his age?* he wondered. *Probably.* But at thirty-nine, with nearly twenty years on the force, he had seen things his most lurid childhood imaginings could not have prepared him for. Wifredo Lam's body, back in 'forty-three, for one. Not that it had been gory— no visible wounds, in fact—but the monstrous getup was what had made it so unsettling.

Fitz had broken up bloody fistfights, taken mutilated knifing victims to the hospital, waited for ambulances to pick up bodies maimed in traffic accidents, cordoned off the mangled remains of jumpers, and even once delivered a baby in the back of a squad car, all part of the job. But something about the Lam killing had gotten under his skin.

It was the disfiguring aspect of it, the deliberate desecration. Even though he was well aware of the costume's actual significance, it mocked the dead man in a way that offended Fitz's sense of decency. Calling it an exquisite corpse made it even more bizarre.

To the Surrealists, who invented the game, that was the point—the more bizarre, the better. Which was fine as long as the corpse was only a drawing. It was another story altogether when it was human.

Fitz's mind returned to the present when they arrived at the cottage, where a note was pinned to the door. *Please call police headquarters, EA4-0024, and ask for Chief Steele,* it read.

"You get TJ out of those fishy clothes and into the outside shower," suggested Nita. "I'll run over to the inn and phone."

She was put through immediately, and the chief made his request without preliminaries. "I'd be much obliged if you and your husband would come to my office right away to discuss the Metzger case." Nita agreed, and the chief gave them directions.

Once again Emily Green was to be pressed into service, over TJ's protests. "Why can't I go with you? I won't be in the way."

"Wouldn't you rather go to the beach?" coaxed Fitz. "I'm sure Mrs. Green can persuade one of the lifeguards to keep an eye on you. Maybe he'll even let you sit up on the bench with him, and blow the whistle if someone swims out too far. That would be a lot more fun than being stuck inside a dingy police station on such a beautiful day." Fitz had no idea whether such a thing would be allowed, but the prospect seemed appealing to TJ, so they took him to the inn and left him in Mrs. Green's care.

"I have a passkey to the cottage," she told them. "So I can let him in to change into his bathing suit and I'll find him a beach towel. You folks get along to town."

Unlike Fitz's imposing Sixth Precinct station house, built in the 1890s when Teddy Roosevelt was police commissioner, or Nita's Twenty-third Precinct on East 104th Street, which looked more like an apartment building than a police station, the East Hampton Town police headquarters on Newtown Lane resembled a small professional office. The waiting room was furnished with a few comfortable chairs, a Motorola FM Dispatcher two-way radio, and a reception desk behind a gated railing.

Instead of a uniformed sergeant behind the desk barking "Yeah, waddaya want," a clerk in civilian clothes, who doubled as the dispatcher, asked politely how he could be of assistance. Nita relayed the summons from the chief, and they were ushered into his office, a pleasant room ventilated by wide-open screened windows and a ceiling fan. No hard wooden chairs or security bars here, they noted.

Chief Harry M. Steele, white-haired and avuncular, wore his authority lightly. A thirty-three-year veteran of the force, he was a Springs native who knew every nook and cranny of his territory, and everyone in it, during the nine months of the year when East Hampton slept. During the high season, from Memorial Day to Labor Day, it was a different story. The town brimmed with strangers, and it was Steele's job to see that those who broke any of the numerous summer rules and regulations paid their fines promptly. Parking violations and speeding tickets accounted for a hefty chunk of his annual budget.

He thanked Nita and Fitz for coming, directed them to chairs with padded seats, and came straight to the point.

"This Metzger business couldn't have happened at a worse time. Not only is it our busiest time of year, when all my officers are coping with traffic and tourists—no disrespect intended—but there's been a rash of auto accidents, with several fatalities. Now it looks like one of them was a homicide. Frankly, we don't have the resources to investigate all the angles on that one, so I'm going to ask for your help. I know you're on vacation, but I'm stuck or I wouldn't impose."

"I'll be glad to help," said Fitz. "As Officer Finch must have told you, the Metzger-Kligman address is in my precinct in the West Village, so I can have inquiries made there. My men can also contact the women's places of employment, and possibly trace the next of kin. One phone call will set that in motion."

"Good. I appreciate your cooperation. If you'll give the number to Fred Tucker out front, he'll put through the call for you." Fitz rose and excused himself.

"I'd like to impose on you as well, Mrs. Fitzgerald," the chief continued. "I'm told you're a detective, so I hope you'll agree to question the Kligman girl when she regains consciousness. There's no detective on my force, and I don't think any of my officers has the right, ah, technique. I think a woman's touch is needed."

"I understand," said Nita, ignoring his unintentional condescension. "And I'm an experienced interrogator. It has to be carefully handled. On the face of it, she and Pollock are both prime suspects in the strangling.

Nita continued. "Let's assume for the sake of argument that Metzger tried to seduce Pollock, and Kligman killed her in a jealous rage. In her condition, she might incriminate herself, say something she'll deny later, when she's not medicated. Or let's say she saw Pollock do it, for reasons unknown—maybe even accidentally while he was drunk—and she doesn't know he's dead, so she tries to protect him, maybe invents some story about an intruder. Or maybe it *was* an intruder. I saw nothing in the house that looked suspicious, but if Metzger interrupted someone prowling around outside, that could account for it."

She sat back and reflected. "Of course this is all speculation. I wonder if Dr. Cooper can rule out the possibility of a woman doing it. He said her windpipe was crushed—that would take serious force. And maybe the size of the neck bruises would tell him how big the killer's hands were."

Steele was impressed. He leaned over and flipped on his intercom. "Fred, do you have the Metzger autopsy report? Yes? Bring it in, will you?" The file arrived promptly, and Nita pulled her chair around the desk so she and Steele could study it together. The photographs showed the injuries clearly.

"Looks like a classic case of deliberate strangulation," Steele observed. "He grabbed her right around the throat and choked her to death."

In addition to a postmortem fracture of the third cervical vertebra and multiple lacerations to the upper body as a result of the car crash, the report described cutaneous bruising and abrasions to the neck, engorged tissues at and above the compression sites, fractured larynx, compressed cricoid cartilage, and ocular petechiae—broken blood vessels in and around the eyes. It also noted manual bruising on the upper arms, and the removal of skin fragments from under the index and middle fingernails on Metzger's right hand.

"She must have fought back, and scratched whoever did it," said Steele. "Let's hope it was on his face. Likely to be a man, isn't it?"

"Considering the amount of force needed to cause those injuries, I think it's safe to assume the killer was male," agreed Nita. "Assuming he came at her from in front— which is what it looks like from the bruise patterns—it's probable that she scratched her killer on the left cheek or neck.

"The right side of Kligman's face was badly abraded," Nita continued, "but when I found her, there were no injuries on the left side. Apparently she was thrown clear of the car and landed on the road, hitting her head on the right side. Dr. Abel can confirm the extent of her other injuries. Dr. Cooper said that Pollock's head wounds were also on the right side. Maybe we can see his autopsy report as well."

"He may not be finished yet. I'll ask Fred to call Yardley and Williams and find out." Steele used the intercom again. While they waited, Nita decided to set him straight on her rank and title.

"You were right about my being a detective," she told him. "I won promotion five years ago. As you can guess, there aren't many female detectives in the NYPD, but I had a wonderful mentor who encouraged me. Hector Morales, the super sleuth of the Twenty-third Precinct. They call him *El Zorro*, you know what that means?" More than a year before the ABC television show of that name began to air, the Spanish term was far from common knowledge, and Steele confessed his ignorance.

"It means 'the fox,' and it's a well-deserved nickname, believe me. His investigative work was crucial to solving the case that brought me and Fitz together back in 'forty-three. He's an inspector now, still based in Spanish Harlem. In some ways the Bonackers remind me of that community—tight-knit, family-oriented, proud of their heritage, hard for outsiders to penetrate. Add to that the language barrier, and you can see how important it is to have local people of all ranks on the force."

She paused, striving to be diplomatic. "That's why I've chosen to keep my maiden name. Off duty I'm proud to be Mrs. Brian Fitzgerald, but when I'm on duty it's Detective Juanita Diaz, though I'd be pleased if you'd call me Nita."

Steele broke out in a broad grin, reached for her hand, and shook it vigorously. "Well, well, I'm glad to know you, Detective Juanita Diaz! I'll be happy to call you Nita if you'll call me Harry."

Nita's satisfaction was interrupted by the intercom.

"The doc has finished with Pollock," Fred told them. "If you want to go over there he'll give you the results in person."

Over there was little more than a crosstown block away, at the other end of Newtown Lane, so Nita, Fitz, and Steele decided not to bother with the car.

"Got pretty much everything we need right here on this street," observed Steele as they strolled west toward the train station. "Dreesen's Excelsior Market for food, Parsons Electric for an icebox to put it in, Diamond's Department Store for a table to eat it off, Dakers' Wines and Spirits for something to wash it down with, Vetault's flower shop to decorate the table, and Halsey's Garage for a Dodge truck to run it all home in. Oh, and East End

Hardware for the garbage pail. And if you'd rather eat out, there's Sam's."

"And when you've had your last meal," quipped Fitz, "Yardley and Williams will take care of the remains." That got a belly laugh out of Steele, and a loud giggle out of Nita.

"Pollock used to bend an elbow at Sam's," Steele told them. "One night a couple years ago, when he'd had one too many—no, make that a few too many—and was causing a ruckus, Sam Nasca kicked him out. Pollock got sore and threw a rock through the front window. When he sobered up he was so apologetic, said he'd pay for the damage, and Sam said *Damn right you will!*

"Spent plenty of time in Cavagnaro's, too," Steele continued. "Up ahead on the other side of Pleasant Lane, opposite the funeral parlor. Albie Cavagnaro told me he stopped in yesterday morning for an eye-opener, on his way to meet the 11:04 from the city. Kind of ironic. He started the day there, and ended it just across the street."

Carolyn Williams admitted the trio and escorted them down to the basement, where Dr. Cooper was waiting.

"Thanks for coming by," he said. "I haven't written up the results yet, and I'm afraid that'll have to wait. I have to get over to Southampton. There was a major accident there last night, outside the Scotch Mist Inn. Head-on collision, eight dead and one critical. Lots of autopsies lined up, so they need all the medics they can get. Another case of drunk driving. This county's record is a disgrace—we really need to step up the safe driving campaign. Anyway, let me fill you in on the Pollock autopsy." He motioned them to chairs.

"Pollock sustained a compound skull fracture causing severe brain lacerations. He also had lacerated lungs and bleeding into the chest cavity caused by a collapsed rib cage. Either of those injuries would have been fatal. They were sustained when his body slammed into the oak tree where you found him, Captain Fitzgerald. He was catapulted out of the car and thrown against the tree. If he'd missed it, he might have survived, but not for long. He was suffering from advanced cirrhosis of the liver, with resultant edema and jaundice. Not a good prognosis, but that's moot now."

"Were there any scratches on the left side of his face or neck?" asked Steele.

"I know what you're getting at, but no, the left side was unmarked. If Metzger scratched her killer on the left face or neck, it wasn't Pollock. All the visible damage was on the right side of his head, and on his right torso, which was covered by his shirt. There was very little external bleeding—the fatal injuries were internal."

NINETEEN.

Saturday, August 11

By eight thirty the sun had been down for half an hour and plans for the evening were still up in the air. Jackson had hardly touched the dinner Ruth had prepared—steak, corn on the cob, and beefsteak tomato salad, followed by apple pie nicely warmed in the oven, with whipped cream on top. In the middle of the meal he suddenly got up from the table, muttered something about needing to feed the dogs, and disappeared out the back door with a couple of cans and a can opener in hand. After a while he came back in and sat silently at the table, chain smoking and refilling his glass with gin over Ruth's protests.

"Please, Jackson, if we're going to the concert, you'll have to drive, so you'd better hold off on that." To which he grimaced and poured himself another hit.

"Let's not go," said Edith. "You don't have to entertain me. I can just watch television, or we can play cards, whatever you like."

Jackson scowled at her. "I told Alfonso we'd be there. I'm fine; don't worry. I'll just take a nap while you girls get ready. Wake me up at nine." He rose and shambled toward the stairs.

"I'll make some coffee," Ruth called after him. "I'll have it all ready for you when you wake up." She turned to her friend apologetically. "I'm sorry, Edie. He just needs rest."

Edith, tired of Ruth's excuses, was losing patience.

"What does he have to rest for? He hasn't done anything all day except mope around, sleep practically the whole afternoon away, then bundle us into the car and haul us off to his friends' house, dump us in the living room and leave us to make small talk with a total stranger. Then when we got back he disappeared into the studio for a couple of hours. Okay, I thought, at least he's doing some work in there, but when we went to get him for dinner he was just sitting there with the dogs at his feet, staring at the wall. With a half-empty gin bottle next to him."

She reached for the pack of Camels he had left on the table and took one for herself. "If you two want to go to the concert, fine, but I'm staying here. I don't want to be in the car with him in that condition."

Ruth was persistent. "You'll see; he just needs to sleep it off. Let's not disappoint him. Finish your cigarette while I clear the table, then we'll go upstairs and make ourselves beautiful." She gathered up some plates and carried them to the sink.

"I'll bet you've never been inside a mansion. That's where we're going, a genuine mansion," Ruth went on with enthusiasm. "It even has a name, not just a number like an ordinary house. It's called The Creeks, because the property has a creek on either side. You drive down a long, winding driveway through beautiful grounds, all landscaped, and pull up to a covered entrance, just like those glamorous house parties in the movies." She hoped that would pique the interest of her film-loving friend.

"Inside," she continued, "the house is full of modern art. The owner, Alfonso Ossorio, is a painter himself, but he's a collector, too. He's rich, so he can buy anything he wants. He has several of Jackson's paintings. I'm hoping I can persuade him to look at some of the things in my gallery. That's another reason to go, to try and soften him up a bit." She was remembering how he had ignored her at the party a couple of weeks ago.

Warming to her topic, Ruth decided to apply some wishful thinking.

"Alfonso knows everybody. I wouldn't be surprised if some of his Broadway and Hollywood friends will be there. Lots of them have summer places out here. Why, I saw Lauren Bacall shopping at the farmer's market in Amagansett last weekend, and I heard Marilyn Monroe and Arthur Miller are staying around there. That's not far away. Maybe they'll come."

That was enough for Edith. She could watch *Two For the Money, People Are Funny,* or Lawrence Welk any Saturday night, but when did she have the chance to socialize with celebrities? Even just seeing them across the room would provide her with excellent stories for her clients at the Beautique Salon on West 57th Street, where she worked as a hairdresser and receptionist.

"All right, Ruth, you win. Here, I'll help you with the dishes and then we'll get changed."

"Leave the dishes, Edie. You go on up while I get the coffee ready."

Walking quietly up the stairs and past the closed door to the guest room where Jackson was sleeping, Edith entered the master bedroom and switched on the light. She glanced at the bathing suit she had left on the chair, wondering whether they would get a chance to swim tomorrow. In anticipation of an evening out, she had brought a charming blue party dress that complemented her eye color. Crossing to the closet, she slipped out of her sundress and exchanged it for the blue one. From the bureau drawer she removed a garter belt and nylons and put them on, then a couple of half slips that fluffed out the skirt nicely. A pair of white pumps, a matching handbag, and a white rayon scarf finished off the outfit.

She sat on the bed nearest the back wall, where a shelf held a portable vanity, and opened her makeup case. Inside, among the cosmetics, was a string of blue glass beads. As she put them around her neck, she glanced at the mirror and was suddenly overwhelmed with emotion. The necklace was a gift from her lover, Nick—ten years older than she, and married, with two young children—who was also her boss at the salon.

"Blue to match your beautiful eyes," he had told her, kissing her neck as he fastened the clasp.

She closed those eyes and savored the memory of his kiss, his touch. But with equal intensity she remembered the agonizing days working in the same room with him but unable to acknowledge their relationship. And the weeks of waiting for the opportunity to steal time together, when he could make some excuse for working late that wouldn't arouse his wife's suspicions.

After more than a year of this secrecy and duplicity she was still deeply in love with him, but had come to the realization that he would never leave his family and marry her. Her eyes opened, and she wiped away the tears that had formed under her lids.

I must be realistic, she said to herself. *When I get back to the city I'll break it off. I can find a job someplace else. Ruth says I should do like she's doing, follow my heart and not care what anyone thinks, but I do care. And my heart is going to break if I don't pull myself together. He says he loves me, but even if that's true, it's not enough.*

Edith squared her shoulders and smiled at her reflection. "That's better," she told the mirror. "Don't be a fool. Face facts and get on with your life."

She found a box of tissues, blew her nose, gave her eyes another wipe, and applied her makeup.

TWENTY.

Ruth stood outside the guest room with the coffee. A gentle tap on the door brought no response.

"Isn't he awake yet?" asked Edith as she emerged from the bedroom.

"Awake or not, I have to go in and get changed," said Ruth. "All my clothes are in the closet in there." She gave Edith an appraising once-over. "You look gorgeous! I love that color on you. Isn't that the necklace Nick gave you? Perfect." She kissed her cheek.

"You go down and I'll get this coffee into him. He can wash up while I get dressed. He has clean clothes in the dresser. There's more coffee on the stove if you want it."

Edith said okay, went downstairs, and turned on the radio, hoping to tune in *Saturday Night Swing* on WNEW but finding only a Rhode Island station playing classical music. *Oh, well,* she thought, *it'll put me in the mood for the concert.*

Ruth opened the guest room door and entered. The room was dark and stuffy, with blinds drawn over the closed windows as if to exclude the world, but she could make out a huddled form on the bed.

She switched on the bedside lamp and saw Jackson curled into a fetal position under the sheet. He groaned and pulled the sheet over his face.

"Wake up, sleepyhead," she cooed as she set the coffee cup on the bedside table. "It's nine o'clock, time to rise and shine." Her simpering was met with a curse as he stretched, grimaced, and blinked his eyes open.

"Fuck the coffee. It's you I want. Come here." A rough hand grasped her wrist and pulled her onto the bed.

"Jackson, not now!" She freed her arm from his grip. "We have to get ready for the concert. Edith is all ready and waiting downstairs."

"Let her wait. I love you, goddammit. I need you." Clumsily, he pulled at the straps of her sundress and fumbled for her breasts. The effort seemed to exhaust him. He lurched forward, buried his face in her lap, and without warning started to sob.

"I'm afraid," he gasped, "help me."

He had pushed the right button. Ruth dissolved into a puddle of concern. "Jackson, darling, what are you afraid of? I won't let anything hurt you. I promise. What do you want me to do?"

"I'm afraid I'll lose you. Help me show you how much

I love you." He pulled back the sheet, revealing his naked body, and placed her hand on his flaccid penis.

"Help me," he whispered.

Ruth felt her nipples contract, sending a stab of desire down to her genitals. A slow smile spread across her face. Now she was in control. The world's greatest artist was begging her to restore his manhood, his self-respect, his genius. And she had the power to do it.

Ignoring his bloated belly and sour breath, she stroked him as she bent over and kissed him deeply on the mouth, and he moaned as he returned her kiss. She kissed him again, lower down this time, then lower still, and felt him begin to harden.

"Watch me," she said. She rose and began to undress, caressing herself as she did so. "I'm pretending you're touching me, arousing me," she teased, while he followed her hands with his eyes.

At one point he actually licked his lips, and she chuckled low in her throat. "I want you to lick my lips. Not the ones on my mouth, the other ones." She stood beside the bed with legs apart and he obliged her, while her hand kept his penis occupied.

When he was fully erect, she pulled back. "Now," she said, "you can do what you want with me. But close your eyes for a minute while I get ready." He grinned and did as he was told, playing with himself and burning with anticipation while she reached into the bureau drawer and took out her diaphragm, applied a dab of cream, and inserted it.

Suddenly she was on top of him, straddling him and groping for his erection. His eyes popped open and he thrilled at the sight of her—young, beautiful, glistening with sweat and panting with desire for him and him alone. She threw back her head and gasped, calling his name softly as he slipped inside her.

His self-pity and despair evaporated, and he felt a surge of hope. *If I can still get it up, still satisfy a sexy girl like this one, then I still have what it takes to paint. Doesn't it all come from the same place? Painting, screwing, it's all about creating. Yes, I can do it; I can do it all!*

Her coffee finished, a couple of cigarettes smoked, and her patience at an end, Edith looked at the kitchen clock with frustration. It said nine thirty. *What the hell is keeping them? The damn concert will be over by the time we get there. Well, maybe that's not so bad. The reception afterward is really what Ruth is looking forward to, and that's when I'll get the chance to rub elbows with the movie stars.*

Even with the back door open, it was hot in the kitchen, so she decided to sit outside on the lawn. It was a pretty night—the crescent moon's reflection dappled the creek, the fireflies were flashing their mating signals, and the katydids chirped cheerfully in the undergrowth.

Edith settled into a lawn chair and began to plan her future.

TWENTY-ONE.

Monday, August 13

At 11:45 a.m. Trans World Airlines Flight 83 landed on schedule at New York International Airport, commonly known as Idlewild, since it was built on the grounds of the Idlewild Beach Golf Course. Alfonso Ossorio and his companion, Ted Dragon, were on hand to meet the plane. As they watched Lee descend the gangway, they steeled themselves for the long drive back to East Hampton with what they assumed would be a basket case.

But when she neared the gate they could see that she looked composed and determined, ready to face the ordeal they all knew was coming. The outpouring of sympathy had already begun, with tributes flowing in from friends and enemies alike. Even Alexander Eliot, *Time* magazine's conservative art editor, who never missed an opportunity to heap scorn on Pollock and his art, had sent his condolences to Lee. Those who viewed Jackson as the killer of an innocent victim—assuming Edith had died in the crash—were maintaining a discreet silence, at least for now.

Alfonso and Ted embraced Lee, wrapping her in their protective blanket of concern. She greeted them gratefully, but with cool reserve.

"Give me your suitcase," urged Ted, relieving her of her hand luggage. "Where are your baggage claim checks? I'll take care of collecting the bags."

"This is it," Lee told him. "I sent my trunk back on the ship. It should arrive next week. Now please take me home." Very efficient, very matter-of-fact, all under control. *My God*, thought Ossorio, *don't underestimate this woman.*

"Everything is arranged," he told her as they walked to his Lincoln sedan. "The funeral is on Wednesday, at the Springs chapel. Paul told me that's where you wanted it."

"That's where Jackson would have wanted it," she snapped. "His people are Presbyterian, although you wouldn't know it. They're actually against religion. But he insisted on a church wedding, so he'll have a church funeral."

"The grave is in Green River Cemetery, as you requested," Ossorio continued. "On that little rise at the back, near the woods."

"Jackson and I walked there often. He said that's where he wanted to be buried, with the Bonackers. He respected them, I can't imagine why. Bunch of inbred hicks."

Ossorio found that attitude offensive, since he considered the Springs natives to be honest, industrious people with deep roots in a community they loved, like the natives of his homeland, the Philippines. But he hesitated to contradict her. *Now is not the time,* he said to himself. *She's prickly even on her good days, and this is certainly not one of them.*

The return drive was made largely in silence. Lee sat alone in the backseat, dismissing Ted's offer to join her. His well-meaning efforts at small talk were ignored, so it wasn't long before he gave up and left her to her thoughts. He was coping with his own distress and sense of loss.

Ted Dragon and Jackson Pollock had grown close in the winter and spring of 1949–50, when Alfonso Ossorio was away in the Philippines for several months. Ted had stayed behind in New York while Ossorio painted a mural for his family's Roman Catholic chapel in Victorias. It was a painful separation for the young ballet dancer, so early in a passionate relationship that had to be kept secret from Alfonso's stern father and deeply pious mother. Jackson had been unexpectedly sympathetic, comforting Ted in a brotherly way, even giving him a painting as a token of friendship. This was a side of Pollock—the kindness, the loyalty, the intuitive caring—that was invisible to people outside his close circle.

For his part, Alfonso had taken courage from Jackson's example, another misfit rebelling against expectations and conventions, struggling with self-doubt one minute and supremely confident the next. Despite their polar differences—Alfonso born rich and Jackson born poor, Alfonso gay and Jackson straight, Alfonso religious and Jackson a nonbeliever—they shared a subjective approach to art that relied on a different kind of faith: the conviction that the artist had something to say that would have meaning beyond his own narrow need to express himself in paint.

But for Lee the loss went far deeper. The years of struggle to gain recognition in an indifferent art world fixated on the School of Paris as the only true innovators, the months of preparation for shows the critics were likely to hate and the collectors likely to ignore, the weeks when her own work was set aside so Jackson's needs could be met, the days spent on the phone with anyone who might be persuaded to take an interest in his work, and the hours of worrying when he was off on a bender or out God knows where in the car.

Fourteen years of all that—with a respite of only those two marvelous years when he was sober and brilliantly productive—had depleted her physically and emotionally, as well as professionally, since she had put her own career on hold to promote his.

Why had she done it? For love, pure and simple. Love for him, and love for his work. And what did she get in return? Betrayal. Beneath her resolute exterior, her bitterness was palpable to empathetic friends like Alfonso and Ted.

So was her guilt. Lee tortured herself with unanswerable questions. What would have happened if she had stayed home, forced his hand? Would he have come to his senses and chosen her over Ruth? Would she have been able to get him back on the wagon before it was too late? Would he have found his way out of the creative impasse that had stalled his career?

Why had she abandoned him when he needed her more than ever? Why did he always drive so recklessly? Why did he have to throw his life away?

Why, for God's sake, why did he have to take another life as well?

TWENTY-TWO.

Over iced tea on the cottage deck later that morning, while TJ played catch in the parking lot with one of the off-duty busboys, Nita and Fitz speculated on how events might have unfolded on Saturday night.

"Where was Pollock coming from? He was driving back home from somewhere," said Fitz. "I assume the local police will check his whereabouts, find out if anyone saw him and the women earlier that evening."

Nita opened up a line of reasoning. "Suppose they were at a party where someone got rough with Metzger, whether it was Pollock or someone else? Maybe she wasn't dead, just unconscious, and he wanted to get her home to recover. Naturally he'd be in a hurry, even more so than usual. Probably a bit panicky, probably not sober. That would account for the speed, and the direction."

"If that were the case," said Fitz, "you'd think someone who was at the party would have come forward. There can't be a soul in the area who doesn't know about the accident by now."

"Weren't they supposed to be going to Ossorio's? That's what he told Dr. Cooper. Evidently they never got there, at least if Ossorio's telling the truth."

"Why wouldn't he?"

"If he's the one who strangled her."

"Ah. But surely some of the other guests would have seen them."

"Yes, that's most likely, unless he headed them off before they could go in."

"Why would he do that?"

Nita had a suggestion. "You remember he said he's loyal to Lee. Suppose he had second thoughts about letting Pollock bring not one but *two* pretty young women to a concert where all his friends, and Lee's, would see them. How would it look, Pollock parading his girlfriends like that? For all Ossorio knew, he was balling them both!"

Fitz nodded. "I see what you're getting at. Maybe he tried to call Pollock, tell him not to come, but they'd already left. So he waits outside for them to arrive, tries to persuade them to leave quietly, but Metzger makes a fuss and he's afraid she'll disturb the concert, so he grabs her by the throat. But he throttles her too hard. She passes out, and Pollock bundles her into the car and takes off, not realizing that her windpipe is crushed and she's dying."

"Ossorio may be a pansy, but he's a big guy. I'd say he's strong enough to have done it the way you describe."

"Yeah, but on the face of it Pollock and Kligman are more likely. Maybe Kligman's a lot stronger than she looks. Pretty hard to tell when she's lying in the road semi-conscious. If she was mad enough, and jealous enough, maybe she'd be capable. What's the old saying, 'Hell hath no fury?'"

"That's a scorned woman, not a jealous one," Nita reminded him, "but it could amount to the same thing if Pollock was putting the make on Metzger without her approval. Which brings up another possible angle." She checked to make sure that TJ was out of hearing range.

"Sexual strangulation. What the medical examiner calls erotic asphyxiation. We had a case once, a few years back. Hector assigned me because the victim was female. Seems she liked her boyfriend to tie her up and tighten a rope around her neck until she almost passed out. For some reason, when the blood supply to the brain is cut off it heightens sexual pleasure."

Fitz's eyebrows went up, and Nita hastened to add, "Don't even think about it. It's very dangerous. Too much pressure, especially with a ligature, and it's all over. That's what happened to our victim, pretty little Puerto Rican girl. The boyfriend tried to cover it up, make it look like suicide, but we arrested him for murder. Fortunately for him she'd told a couple of her girlfriends about being a gasper—that's what they call people who get off that way—and encouraged them to try it. They testified, the boyfriend changed his story, and the jury believed him."

Fitz's imagination was working overtime. "Maybe Metzger was a gasper. Maybe Pollock was doing both women, Kligman the regular way and Metzger with a stranglehold."

Nita was skeptical. "That seems pretty far-fetched to me. According to Doc Cooper, Pollock was in really bad shape physically. I wonder if he was even capable of doing it the regular way."

"All the more reason why he might have been willing to experiment with Metzger," reasoned Fitz. "It could be a real turn-on."

"Down, boy," she cautioned. "Let's not get carried away. I only suggested it as a possibility because she died of asphyxia. Obviously she was strangled, but why? And why were they headed home? Whatever happened must have happened somewhere else, but where?"

As they pondered these questions, a messenger from the inn came to tell them that Fitz was wanted on the phone. "You can take it in Mr. Bayley's office," he said.

The innkeeper was cooperation personified. "Please feel free to treat my office as your own, Captain Fitzgerald. The telephone is at your disposal, no extra charge. Harry Steele asked me to give you every assistance. He's very grateful for your help on this case."

Bayley left the room as Fitz lifted the receiver, certain that the switchboard operator was listening in.

"Fitzgerald here," he said. "Who's calling?"

"Hello, Captain, this is Murphy at the Six. We got information on those two women you wanted us to trace."

He sat down at the desk and found a pencil and note pad. "Let's have it."

"They were roommates, all right. Shared one of the four apartments in that building. The landlady insisted on getting the names and addresses of their families, in case they skipped out on the rent. Said she'd had a couple of bad experiences with single women doing a vanishing act. Anyway, if you're ready I'll give you the dope."

Fitz took down the details, thanked Murphy for the good work, and rang off. Kligman's mother and sister lived in New Jersey, and Metzger's mother and brother were in the Bronx. Apparently both fathers were either dead or missing.

He fished Chief Steele's card out of his shirt pocket, asked for an outside line, and dialed the number. The clerk put him through, and he relayed the information. He also mentioned that he was calling from the Sea Spray office, confident that Steele would realize the call was going through the switchboard.

Steele took the hint and guarded his remarks. "Thank you very much, Captain Fitzgerald. Now comes the hard part. I hate to inform these folks over the phone, but I can't spare anyone to go in person."

"If you're agreeable," Fitz suggested, "I'll get one of my men to do it. Or a woman, if you think that would be better. Why don't I come by the office and we can discuss it in person?" No way was he going to talk about Metzger's death on an open line.

He agreed to go at once, and returned to the cottage to tell Nita what was happening.

"I won't be long. If you and TJ want to run into the village with me, you can pick up some lunch at Dreesen's while I meet with the chief. And I sure wouldn't mind if you bought a bag of their homemade donuts. We can have them for breakfast tomorrow—if they last that long."

TWENTY-THREE.

"Maybe we should have walked," said Fitz with dismay as he tried in vain to find a parking space on Newtown Lane. Both sides of the street were lined with cars, and the sidewalks were filled with shoppers and strollers. "Now I know where all the folks from Brooklyn and Queens go in the summer," he observed drily.

"Manhattan, too, including us," added Nita. "Though the sidewalks here are just as hot as in the city. I prefer the cottage and the beach. The ocean is a natural air conditioner."

"I'll get you back there as soon as I can," said Fitz. He did a U-turn at the railroad tracks and headed back toward Main Street. Luckily for them a space opened up in front of the hardware store, and he pulled in.

"Come to the police station when you finish shopping," he told Nita. "If I'm done first I'll wait there for you."

Fred Tucker showed Fitz into the office, where the

chief thanked him for coming. "I really hate to impose on you like this, Captain Fitzgerald," he said. "Not much of a vacation for you, is it?"

"Please call me Fitz," he replied, "and don't think anything of it. I'm glad to help you out. After all, my men are doing all the legwork. I'm just the messenger boy."

"That's mighty decent of you," said the chief. "I'll write out instructions for your officers so the families can get in touch with me to follow up. I think it would be advisable to send a female officer, if that's possible. It'll be hard enough on Mrs. Kligman to find out that her girl is in the hospital in bad shape, but nothing like as bad as it'll be for Mrs. Metzger."

Fitz waited while Steele worked out some wording, adding his own name and number, Southampton Hospital contact information for Mrs. Kligman, and the funeral home for Mrs. Metzger.

"From what you gave me," he told Fitz, "there's no Mr. Metzger in the picture, so maybe she's a widow, or divorced. I hope the brother's older, so he can take care of the arrangements. Unfortunately we can't release the body until we figure out who killed her. Carolyn Williams will know how to handle it. She's aware of the situation, but she's not one to go blabbing. If she were the gossiping sort, Yardley and Williams would be out of business in a hurry."

Fitz used the chief's phone and got through to the Sixth Precinct. "Is Officer Kelly on duty?" he asked Sergeant

Murphy. "Good. Ask her to take the Jersey visit first. The Bronx one will be harder. Think she can do them both today? If not, Metzger can wait until tomorrow. No urgency there, I'm afraid."

"Any more word on Kligman?" asked Fitz after he hung up.

"I called the hospital just before you got here," Steele told him. "She's in and out of consciousness, still sedated but apparently out of danger. Fortunately nothing broken, no organ damage, but she's pretty banged up. Bruises all over her body, and a concussion. Doc Abel is keeping an eye on her. He thinks she'll be coming around any time now."

"Nita will be available to question her whenever she's ready. If we're at the cottage or on the beach Mr. Bayley can get a message to us, and if we go anywhere else I'll check in with you first."

"By the way," said Steele, "thanks for tipping me about calling from the Sea Spray office phone. There's no way Millie Dayton wasn't listening in. If I call you there I won't let anything slip."

"Nita and I were kicking around a few ideas," Fitz told him. "Probably nothing you haven't already thought of," he added diplomatically.

"Mind sharing them?"

Fitz summarized their conversation, and the chief listened with interest.

"You're right, we did check on various places where

Pollock and the girls might have been spotted earlier in the evening. Apparently they went straight back to Springs after they left the Brooks place in Montauk. It's a nineteen-mile drive, and we canvassed all the shops and bars along the way. Nobody saw them. Earlier in the day Dreesen's delivered groceries to the house, and it looks like they had dinner when they got back.

"After that, any of the three possibilities you and Nita discussed could have happened. Pollock gets liquored up, makes a pass at Metzger, Kligman gets sore and goes for her. That's the least likely, in my opinion. First of all, I don't think Kligman's strong enough to have killed her that way. Plus the only scratches on her face are on the right side, where her face hit the pavement.

"And I'm not partial to the sex thing—not that I have any experience with a case like that. But let's just say that's what happened. She'd probably be naked, so they'd have to put something on her to take her to the hospital. But why get her all dressed up in underwear and a party dress? Why not just throw on a coat or a robe to cover her up? And if bondage is part of it, where are the rope marks, and for that matter where's the rope? On top of that, they were driving toward home, not toward Southampton. No, I just don't buy it.

"The Ossorio idea, on the other hand, seems much more plausible. That would explain why they were headed north on Fireplace Road. They were taking her home, hoping she'd recover, but she died on the way. Doc

Cooper says there's no way to tell for sure how long she'd been dead before the crash, but she was alive long enough for bruises and petechiae to appear—they don't come up after death, because there's no blood circulation. He says with the degree of pressure used on her throat they'd show very quickly. It's seven miles from The Creeks to the crash site. Even going fifty flat out all the way it would take him nearly ten minutes, plenty of time.

"But however it happened," he concluded, "Kligman will know. We have to assume she was there."

TWENTY-FOUR.

By the time the Fitzgerald family returned to the cottage all three of them were wiping powdered sugar off their shirtfronts, and the number of Dreesen's donuts in the bag had decreased from a dozen to six.

Gorging on those treats had successfully deflected TJ's attention from the investigation. Still in the dark about the details of Metzger's death, he nevertheless was eager to know why his parents were helping the East Hampton Town police.

Fitz explained that the women's apartment was in his precinct, and told him about the chief's request that Nita question Kligman when she came to.

"Just because we're off duty doesn't mean we stop being cops," he said. "This is a small force here, no detective, and it's the busy season, as you can tell. They have their hands full even without two deaths and a serious injury. I know they'd do the same for us if the situation was reversed."

"Let's get these groceries into the kitchen and I'll fix us some lunch," said Nita, "or maybe those donuts were enough."

Her two men looked at each other as if to say, *Is she kidding?* She took the hint, and chuckled indulgently.

"Of course not. What was I thinking? All right, sit down while I make sandwiches. And here's some fruit if you can't wait. There's cold pop in the icebox."

With lunch over and the remaining donuts safely stashed away, Fitz suggested an afternoon on the beach.

"What do you say about heading to the beach, buddy?" he asked TJ, who replied with enthusiasm, "Yeah! I want to go body surfing! I saw them doing it yesterday."

"We have to wait an hour before we go in," his father cautioned. "But we can build another sand castle in the meantime. And some of the other kids will probably be down there, too." In addition to the families in the cottages, there were several in the inn itself, which even fed their youngsters in a separate children's dining room.

"I hope the same lifeguard is there today," said TJ. "He let me climb up on the bench with him, and told me all about how they learn to save people from drowning. And how to body surf."

"You'd both better put some zinc oxide on your noses," Nita advised as they changed into their swimsuits. She dabbed some on her own nose. "You're going to look like boiled lobsters if you don't cover up more. I have my sun hat, and I'm going to keep my robe on when I'm not in the water. Just look at these freckles!" She pointed to her cheeks, at which Fitz and TJ burst out laughing.

"You call those freckles? That's nothing. Look at the two of us and you'll see real freckles." It was true, they were both covered head to toe. Fitz was especially proud of his crop. "What's a redheaded Mick without freckles?" he boasted.

Nita's heart melted at the sight of her husband and son admiring each other's sun-spotted skin. The boy certainly was a chip off the old block, more Timothy than Juan, for sure. His first name came from Fitz's father, and his middle name honored her late father, a Cuban immigrant who was killed in a bank robbery in 1936, when she was eighteen. That was what had motivated her to join the police force, in spite of the dual obstacles of her sex and her Hispanic heritage.

In 1938 she was among the nearly five thousand women who took the first civil service exam for the rank of Policewoman, and was one of only three hundred who passed it. By now there were more female and minority officers, though it was even harder for women to get in than it had been in her day. A college degree was now required, while she had entered with only a high school diploma.

Being a fluent Spanish speaker was essential at the Twenty-third Precinct, in the heart of Spanish Harlem.

She was also fortunate in befriending Detective Hector Morales, *El Zorro*, who had taught her the fine points of investigation, evidence gathering, and interrogation, a detective's three indispensable skills.

When she'd reached her thirtieth birthday she had decided it was now or never, and told Fitz she was ready to start a family; but she'd been afraid she'd lose both seniority and respect. "Don't worry," Morales had assured her, "your place here is safe, and you can use your time off to study up for your promotion." As the proud father of three, he should know perfectly well that having a baby was not time off—as in a relaxing leave of absence—but, grateful for his support, she didn't contradict him.

But even more important than Hector's backing was the willingness of her mother, Blanca, to act as TJ's babysitter. Nita would drop him off each morning at her apartment, only a few blocks from the precinct house, and pick him up on her way home. In the baby carriage and later in the stroller he went everywhere with Blanca, whose girlfriends fussed over him and called him *lindo niño pelirrojo*, cute redheaded boy. When he grew into an energetic toddler, she took him to the playground and the park. If a case kept Nita late, no problem—Blanca was only too happy to have him for the duration.

"He's a perfect little angel," she would tell her daughter in Spanish. "Never a moment's trouble." Nita doubted the truth of that, but she recognized it as her mother's way of affirming the commitment to help her pursue her career. It gave her five years' grace, until TJ started kindergarten, where his ability to curse in two languages made him something of a celebrity.

TWENTY-FIVE.

It was nearly four o'clock when Ossorio's Lincoln turned off Fireplace Road and parked beside Lee and Jackson's house. A mile to the south, as the car had rounded the curve, Alfonso couldn't help seeing the skid marks, and hoped Lee hadn't noticed them. Thankfully she seemed to be paying no attention to anything en route, only breaking the silence twice during the three-hour drive from the airport.

Alfonso had said the funeral was scheduled for Wednesday. She had asked what time, and was told four-thirty p.m. Later, she had asked if her mother had been notified. "No," said Ted, "we thought you'd want to do that yourself." "Yes," she'd replied, and lapsed into si-lence again.

When the car came to a stop Ted hopped out to open the back door for her, but she got there ahead of him, suitcase in hand. It was a small but characteristic gesture of self-reliance—she never waited for a man to hold the door for her or to pull out her chair in a restaurant. "I can manage," she'd say, or "I'll do it myself."

Lee carried her suitcase to the back door, and placed it on the cast-iron garden bench that sat on the porch while she searched in her handbag for the key.

She had brought the little bench with her from the city when she and Jackson had moved to Springs. If she were having an especially rough time with him, more and more in the past year, she would come outside and sit on the bench to calm down.

It reminded her of her life before Jackson, of her apartment on East Ninth Street, where the bench sat under a tall oval mirror in which she would admire herself in the chic outfits she wore in those days. It reminded her of the parties with friends from the Hans Hofmann School of Art, where she was one of the most accomplished pupils. It reminded her of the days when she had supported herself, even as a student working part-time as a model and a waitress. Later, when the WPA Federal Art Project came along, she pulled down a regular paycheck like any other respected professional and rose to the rank of supervisor.

But most of all it reminded her of Igor, her handsome White Russian boyfriend, with whom she had shared the Ninth Street apartment in the 1930s. He had found the bench on the street and lugged it up three flights of stairs. He called it a love seat, just big enough for the two of them. They were a couple for nearly ten years, and she sometimes wondered how different her life would have been if she had married him instead of Jackson. Not that such a thing was likely—his aristocratic émigré family, proudly Russian Orthodox, had no use for her, the daughter of a Jewish fishmonger from the shtetl.

Besides, in those days she thought marriage was an outmoded bourgeois custom, that the word "wife" always had "house" attached to the front of it, and she had no intention of falling into that trap. And frankly, as charming and debonair as Igor could be, he wasn't the world's greatest catch. He was feckless, he drank too much, and he was serially unfaithful to her, sometimes bragging about his conquests right in front of her. After she had protested once too often, he moved out and expected her to forward his things at her expense. That's the kind of nerve he had or, as her family would say, *chutzpah.*

She supposed she should call Igor, let him know about the funeral. He and Jackson weren't on the best of terms—he used to show up from time to time and take her for a stroll down Memory Lane, just to get Jackson's goat—but it might be a comfort to have him around. Then again, maybe not. He'd probably get tight and start bragging about what a terrific lover he had been, and would be again now that Jackson was out of the picture—not that she had any intention of taking up with him again. She finally decided not to risk having to put him in his place in front of her family and friends.

There were a lot of other people she needed to call, and

one of the first would be Gerry Weinstock, her lawyer. He was a loyal friend as well as an attorney, and she knew she could trust him to safeguard her interests. His in-laws had a house just down the road, where he and his wife, Margaret, could often be found on long summer weekends. Maybe they were out now, but even if they were back home in Mamaroneck, she wanted Gerry at the funeral. As determined as she was to take charge, she realized she couldn't handle everything alone.

Her brother Irving had to be there, too. The eldest, and the only boy, among the six Krasner children, he was the one person in the world she could completely rely on. Twelve years her senior, he was always there for her, even when they were kids growing up in Brooklyn. He would get up off his deathbed to help her, she was certain. If things hadn't turned out like this, he would have dealt with that little bitch. Too bad she wasn't the one who broke her neck.

What about Lee's mother, Anna? Irving could rent a car and pick her up on his way out. On the other hand, maybe it would be better if she didn't come. She was elderly and frail, and had never been the warm, comforting type. She wouldn't know anyone, and the whole Pollock clan was likely to show up, which would just intimidate her.

So many things to think about, so much to do, and she was so tired. The taxi to the airport in Paris, the tedious wait until her flight was called, nearly twelve hours in the air, and the one-hundred-mile drive from Idlewild, not to mention the six-hour time difference, had taken their toll. She wanted nothing more than to collapse into bed, but that was not going to happen.

Ted had managed to get hold of the small suitcase and he carried it inside as they entered. Cile had done her work well. The house was neat and tidy, everything in place, no indication that anyone other than Jackson and Lee had ever been in residence. But it was unnaturally quiet.

"Where are the dogs?" Lee asked.

"Cile took them up to her place," said Ted. "She thought they'd be better off there than here alone." Lee understood and approved. Gyp, the mongrel, mostly border collie, that had adopted them not long after they moved in, and Ahab, a purebred standard poodle that was a gift from Alfonso and Ted, were deeply attached to Jackson. They sat with him for hours in the studio, patiently waiting for him to start working but indifferent to his idleness, never nagging or complaining like Lee. They accompanied him on long walks in the woods or down to the beach at the end of Fireplace Road, where he would throw sticks out into Gardiner's Bay for them to retrieve. In his absence they needed companionship, which Cile and her husband, Sheridan, could provide. And while she was attached to them herself, she was glad to have one less thing to worry about and two fewer mouths to feed.

"I hope she and Sherry can keep them for a few days,"

said Lee. "It would be better to have them out of the house after the funeral. I'm sure there will be a lot of people coming back. I'll have to see about getting some food."

"For Christ's sake, Lee, let us take care of that," said Ted, somewhat exasperated. Why did she have to act so damned independent? Why was she trying so hard? Of course he knew it was a way of distracting herself from the grief and pain and anger, but it wasn't healthy to be so bottled up. Still, she couldn't afford to fall apart now, not with the whole art world watching.

She was in the spotlight and she knew it. What was it Jackson used to say? That he felt like a clam without a shell. Lee would never let herself be that vulnerable. She had created an armor-plated shell to protect herself, and she was going to need it.

TWENTY-SIX.

Tuesday, August 14

"We couldn't have been luckier with the weather," remarked Fitz as he leaned back in his rocking chair and propped his feet on the deck railing. Nita slipped into a chair beside him, and together they enjoyed the cool morning breeze that swept in from the ocean. The dune in front of the cottage blocked their view of the water, but the relentless throbbing of waves on the sand was a constant audible reminder that they were at the seaside.

Their breakfast of fresh farm eggs and homemade pork sausage from Dreesen's, followed by coffee and the remaining donuts, had been a leisurely affair. TJ, a bit frustrated by his parents' slow start to the morning, was eager to get back into the surf, but Nita wasn't going to be rushed.

"Just hold your horses, young man," she ordered. "Your dad and I have some planning to do. We'll get to the beach before too long, don't worry. Meanwhile, why don't you run over to the inn and see what the other kids are up to? Maybe there'll be a softball game, you don't want to miss that."

Effectively distracted, TJ went to his room to retrieve his glove. He stopped for a moment to admire the Pollock print, which he'd tacked to the wall over his bed. *Sure looks like a lizard to me,* he said to himself. *Lots of other funny-looking things in there, too.* He liked the way it puzzled him, like a visual guessing game. *Plenty of time to study it later,* he thought. He grabbed the glove and headed out while Nita and Fitz settled down to enjoy their second cup of coffee in peace.

"I didn't notice any scratch marks on Ossorio," he said, "but then I wasn't looking for anything like that when we met him. Still, I think I would remember if his face had been scratched."

"I'm sure there was nothing," Nita agreed. "But, you know, she might have scratched her killer's arm or hand, trying to get him to release his grip. Marks like that would be much less obvious. Or, as a matter of fact, she could have scratched herself while she was clawing at him. Do you think there was enough under her nails to get a blood type?"

"I wonder whether Cooper thought of that," said Fitz. "I don't suppose he's done many autopsies. From what the chief said, they haven't had a murder around here in years."

"Maybe not, but there must be plenty of accidental

deaths. How many did he say died on the roads last weekend—eight, wasn't it, not counting Pollock and Metzger? Seems like drunk driving is a blood sport out here. And I'm sure there are at least a couple of drownings every summer, what with all the city folks who don't know how treacherous the open ocean can be, not to mention the inexperienced boaters. Heart attacks, strokes, people choking on food, all those things can happen any time."

"You're right. These country doctors probably get more than their fair share of autopsies. And the fact that Cooper realized that the broken neck didn't kill her, and actually found the skin under her nails, shows he didn't do a superficial job. I wonder if he's tried to run a blood test. I guess they'll have Pollock's blood type. He'd be the first one they'd want to eliminate."

"But he had no scratches on the left side of his face or neck."

Fitz continued to examine the possibilities. "No, but suppose he grabbed her from behind. If she reached back with her right hand, she would have scratched the right side of his face, and those wounds would have been masked by his later injuries."

"Damn," said Nita. "I should have thought of that. Some detective I am! Hector would have my shield if he knew."

"I promise not to tell, but it's gonna cost ya," Fitz teased. "Price: a kiss. Terms: immediate payment."

Nita shrugged. "You drive a hard bargain, but what choice do I have?" She shifted from her rocker to his lap and paid him in full, with interest.

Struggling to keep himself from sweeping her up and carrying her to their bedroom, he contented himself with burying his face in her hair, still damp from her morning shower and smelling of Lustre-Creme, the shampoo of choice for famous redheads like Rita Hayworth and Maureen O'Hara. He brushed her curls aside and kissed her neck as she snuggled closer.

"Besides," said Fitz to make her feel better, "it isn't exactly a foregone conclusion. I'm not even sure the marks on her throat could have been made from behind. But all this guesswork will be over once Kligman comes to. Surely she knows what happened."

For the time being there was nothing more to be said. They lapsed into silence, each trying to put the case aside and concentrate on this moment of intimacy. The natural beauty all around them—the dune grass waving in the sea breeze, the refreshing salty tang in the air, the murmur of the waves against the shore, the cloudless blue sky—and the pleasant sound of children's laughter from the beach just beyond their shaded deck were barely perceived as they focused on each other.

Only a few more days and they'd be back in the city, dealing with the bar fights, gang rumbles, domestic disputes, and other consequences of tempers shortened by the summer heat. Burglaries rose, too, since people left their windows open all day and forgot to close them when they went out.

This far east it was at least ten degrees cooler, and you could leave your windows and doors open all day and night without worrying—though, cops to the core, Fitz and Nita were not about to drop their prudent urban habits just because they were on vacation in the country. When they went out, everything was locked up tight, including the car whenever Fitz parked it.

"Hey, you guys, stop smooching!" TJ had caught them in the act. Startled, they sat up and looked momentarily embarrassed, then grinned at their son as he scolded his father, using a phrase he'd learned from Grandma Blanca. "*¡Qué malo eres, Papá!* Behave yourself!"

Fitz pleaded innocent. "It's not my fault, buddy. Your mom threw herself at me, and I just couldn't resist."

Nita rose, straightened her dress, and tried to reclaim her dignity, but failed. She pointed at her husband. "Pants on fire!" she exclaimed, and all three of them broke out laughing.

When they had composed themselves, TJ delivered a message. "Mr. Bayley asked me to tell you that Chief Steele called. He said the lady in the hospital is conscious, and he wants Mom to question her."

"Of course," replied Nita, suddenly serious. "Now maybe we'll find out what happened to Edith. I'd better go return that call."

TWENTY-SEVEN.

When she got back to the cottage, Nita informed them that a patrol car would come to drive her to Southampton Hospital.

"You guys are on your own for a while," she said. "If you're out when I get back I'll just wait here for you, or maybe take a swim."

TJ said he'd walk over to the inn to see what the other kids were doing. Nita ducked inside the cottage to collect her purse just as her ride arrived. The familiar face of Earl Finch was visible in the driver's seat.

"That was quick," said Fitz. "He must have been on the way already."

"Howdy," Finch called from behind the wheel. Fitz strolled over to the car and returned the greeting.

"Think you have a break in the case?" he asked.

"I sure hope so. Metzger's mother wants us to release the body. The family's Jewish, and they bury their dead right away. Poor woman. She was upset enough before the chief told her she couldn't claim the remains just yet."

"What about the son? Isn't he handling the arrangements?"

"He's only eighteen. He's in bad shape, too. He and his sister were both born in Germany—that's where the family's originally from. The chief got their story. They escaped from the Nazis just in time—fortunately they had relatives here. Only the father didn't get out. He was a college professor. He stayed behind to settle their affairs and got caught. He died in a concentration camp."

"Jesus, that's terrible. Your husband's murdered, and then your only daughter—does she know that, by the way?"

"Yes, the chief had to tell her. Otherwise why not let her have the body? Although he didn't actually use that word. He said the death was suspicious, and that an investigation was under way."

Nita arrived, kissed her husband, and slid into the passenger seat. Calling "See you later," she waved goodbye as Finch left the parking lot and turned up Ocean Avenue toward the highway.

As they headed west into the hamlet of Wainscott, Finch pointed out an imposing gate on their left.

"That's the entrance to The Creeks," he told her, "Ossorio's estate. That's where they had the concert on Saturday night."

"The one Pollock and the girls were supposed to be going to?"

"Right. Too bad you can't see it from the road. It's quite a place. To get a good view of it you really need to be in a boat on Georgica Pond. It looks right out over the water. I used to go there as a kid, when the Herters owned it. Ever hear of the Herter Brothers?" Finch asked.

Nita said no.

"Fancy furniture makers and decorators in New York. Plenty of family money. One of the sons, Albert, was an artist. Him and his wife—she was an artist, too—built the place. It's what rich folks call a summer cottage. Pretty grand for a cottage. Big stucco house, carriage house, boathouse, art studios for both of 'em, fancy gardens all laid out just so, the works. Me and my pals would row over to the dock, and Mrs. Herter would give us ginger ale and cookies. Their two sons were grown and gone, one of 'em was killed in the first war, and I think she missed having boys around the house.

"She died not long after I got back from the army, 'forty-six I think it was, and then her husband died a few years later. The son who lived inherited the place. He's a big-shot politician, the governor of Massachusetts, and he didn't want it. There's something like sixty acres of property to keep up, the house is kind of a white elephant, and he lives in the governor's mansion in Boston, so he put it on the market.

"Lucky for him, a year or so later along comes Ossorio, another artist with plenty of family money, and he buys it. Studios all ready for him, didn't even have to renovate.

I haven't been inside since, but I hear it's full of the abstract art he collects and some weird stuff from France made by hermits and people in the nuthouse."

"Sounds like fun," quipped Nita. "What's his own work like?"

"It's all jumbled up, sorta like Pollock's, only with figures. Course Pollock did figures, too, but that's not what he's known for. Both of 'em show at Guild Hall, the white brick building opposite the library on Main Street. They have art shows and theatricals and club meetings, all kinds of social activities."

"I remember seeing it. We should pay a visit before we leave."

"There's an art show on there right now, and Pollock's in it. Opened just before he got killed. I bet the smart money'll snap up his pictures now that he's dead." That comment was accompanied by a snicker.

"Anyway," Finch continued, "Ossorio's stuff has a lot of religious symbols in it. He's Catholic and so am I, so I recognize some of 'em, but most of it's too obscure for me, and some of it's downright grotesque. Not my cuppa tea. Maybe it's his Spanish heritage—no offense, Nita."

"Certainly not," she hastened to reassure him, "I know what you mean. Some of those old Spanish churches are pretty ornate. Not that I have any firsthand experience, I've only seen pictures. Never been to Spain, never even been to Cuba, where my family's from. I'd love to go, and take my *mamacita*. She left when she was just a kid. But she wouldn't go back now, not while Batista's in power. You can't even say his name in her house."

Their conversation had taken them through Wainscott, Sagaponack, Bridgehampton, Water Mill and into Southampton, where the highway veered off to the right and their route became Hampton Road. A left on Osborne Avenue led to Meeting House Lane and the hospital.

Finch pulled up to the main entrance. "I'll come in with you," he said, "but I'll stay out of the way. Don't want my uniform to spook her."

In the lobby they were directed to the inpatient rooms on the second floor, where the nurse on duty told them that Miss Kligman was in room 208. Finch took a seat in the waiting area while Nita made her way down the hall.

As she approached the room, she stopped suddenly and gasped in amazement. Standing in the doorway, in conversation with Dr. Abel, was Ruth Kligman, apparently completely recovered. Her hair was pulled back off her face, which showed no signs of injury. She was standing unaided, no crutches or cane, and her sleeveless blouse and knee-length skirt revealed no bandages on her unmarked bare arms and legs.

Nita couldn't believe her eyes. Two days ago this woman had been nearly comatose, suffering from concussion and who knew what other internal injuries, and here she was up and about like nothing had happened to her. It was astonishing, and Nita's jaw dropped as she tried to make sense of it.

Just then Dr. Abel spotted her.

"Ah, Detective Diaz, there you are. Chief Steele called to tell me you were on the way. Come, let me introduce you."

Still stunned, she approached the doctor, eyeing his companion warily.

"Thank you for doing this," he began. "I think it's important for a woman to handle the questioning. Ruth is still not very responsive." This confused Nita even further.

"I want you to meet her sister, Iris," he continued, "her identical twin."

Now the mystery of the miraculous recovery was solved.

"She arrived this morning from New Jersey. Iris, this is Detective Juanita Diaz of the New York City Police Department. She's here with her family on vacation, but she's kindly agreed to help with the investigation."

Iris greeted Nita warmly, taking her hand and gazing at her earnestly.

"I can't tell you how much I appreciate your help," she began. "I understand you took care of Ruth at the accident scene, before Dr. Abel got there. He said you knew just what to do—I'm so grateful." Tears formed in her eyes. "I'm the older one, born ten minutes before her. She's my baby sister." The tears rolled down her cheeks, and she fumbled in her skirt pocket for a handkerchief.

The doctor tried to comfort her. "Don't worry, she'll be fine. She just needs rest and quiet. As I explained, the concussion is the most serious injury, but she's over the worst of it." He turned to Nita. "Her whole body is bruised, but remarkably there are no broken bones. I have her on an intravenous painkiller, so she's a bit groggy. You can see her now." He stepped aside and followed the two women into the room.

An IV drip was attached to Ruth's left arm, which was swollen and turning livid as the bruising progressed, but apart from the tape that held the needle in place she was unbandaged. Ointment had been applied to her facial abrasions—Dr. Abel believed that exposing such wounds to the air speeded healing and minimized scarring. Her vacant expression brightened a bit when she saw her sister, and she raised her right hand weakly. Iris held it and patted it fondly as Abel pulled up bedside chairs for her and Nita, then withdrew quietly to a corner of the room.

"Ruthie, honey, this is the lady who helped you when you got hurt," Iris explained. "Do you remember her?"

Ruth let out a shallow sigh. She tried to focus on Nita's face, but couldn't concentrate. When her voice came, it was thin and raspy.

"No, I don't."

"What do you remember?" asked Nita.

Ruth groaned slightly and tried to shift her position in the bed. Suddenly she seemed restless. She tried to push herself up on her elbows, and Abel stepped over to the bed and settled her. He adjusted the drip.

"Where's Jackson? Where is he? What happened to him?"

Nita glanced at Abel, looking for guidance, but his expression was neutral. Apparently Ruth didn't know he was dead. *Funny,* Nita thought, *she's not asking about Edith, only Jackson. I'd better tell her,* she decided. *If I'm evasive or lie to her she won't trust me. She may already be imagining the worst anyway.*

She leaned over and put a hand on Ruth's shoulder. "I'm sorry," she said softly, "he didn't make it."

Ruth's face contorted into a mask of pain. She made a whining noise and gulped for air, trying to sob but failing to fight through the morphine.

"Oh, God, I knew it," she moaned. "Oh, God, Jackson, oh, no . . ." Her voice tailed off. Iris stroked her brow and murmured encouragement, knowing there was no real comfort for her.

Presently her breathing slowed and she became calmer—the drug was doing its work. Unfortunately it made Nita's task harder. She probed gently, hoping for a revelation.

"Do you remember the car going off the road?"

"Yes, it swerved into the woods. Then I woke up here." She gulped again. "And Jackson is dead!"

"Why was he driving so fast?"

"I don't know. He always drives fast." Her head lolled to the left, and it seemed she might fall asleep, but she pulled back and made an effort to pay attention.

"Where were you coming from?"

"I don't remember."

Now Nita had to ask the crucial question.

"What happened to Edith?"

"Edith?"

"Edith Metzger, your roommate. She was in the car with you and Jackson."

"Was she? I don't remember."

"What's the last thing you do remember before the crash?"

Ruth closed her eyes. When she opened them, they brimmed with tears. Her voice was so soft that Nita strained to hear her.

"I remember," she whispered, "making love to Jackson."

TWENTY-EIGHT.

"This kind of short-term memory loss is not uncommon with concussion, especially when it's accompanied by gross physical injury," said Abel as he escorted Nita from the room. Iris stayed behind, reassuring her sister that everything would be all right, which of course it wouldn't. Not that her words really mattered, as Ruth was drifting into drug-induced sleep.

"It's the mind's way of protecting her from emotional distress that could send her back into shock," he explained. "In order to heal she needs to stay calm. Blocking out the traumatic event helps that process. You saw how she reacted when she got a flashback to the car veering off the road. We need to avoid that kind of agitation for the present. I hope you understand." Reluctantly, Nita agreed.

"The last clear memory she has," continued Abel, "is something positive, and it's true, she'd had recent sexual intercourse. She was wearing a diaphragm, which we removed, and we found traces of semen in her vagina. Her memory of what occurred after that will come back in time, when she's better able to cope."

"I sure hope it'll be soon," said Nita. "She's the only person alive who knows what happened to Edith—although that's not necessarily true if it wasn't Pollock who killed her. And if that's the case, there's a live murderer out there and we need to find him."

Abel agreed with her supposition. "I think you're safe in assuming it was a man, whether Pollock or someone else. Dr. Cooper shared the autopsy report with me, and we concur that Kligman doesn't have the strength to inflict those injuries manually."

Remembering her earlier conversation with Fitz, Nita asked, "Can you tell whether the killer grabbed her throat from in front or behind?"

"Not for certain," the doctor told her. "Either way, the lateral bruises on the neck would be more or less the same, depending on the angle of the killer's hands. If he was tall, coming at her from behind would put downward pressure on the neck and throat, which would be just as lethal as a frontal attack, and leave similar marks."

"The reason I ask," she explained, "is that if Edith scratched her attacker's face with her right hand and he was behind her, the scratches would be on the right side, or even on his right hand or arm if she was clawing at it. If it was Pollock, the right side of his face was so badly injured that any earlier scratches wouldn't show, would they?"

"No, they wouldn't. The autopsy report doesn't mention any scratches on his right hand or arm, though."

"Was Dr. Cooper able to get a blood type from the tissue under her nails?"

"Not yet. He had to send the sample to the lab in Riverhead, and the results haven't come back. It was easier with Pollock and Kligman. We drew blood and tested it. Turns out she's Type O positive, very common, but he's unusual, Type A negative. Only seven percent of Caucasians have it."

"Gosh, that would narrow it down," said Nita. "If the skin sample matches Pollock, it makes him the likely killer. Still, it's not definitive. Someone else with that blood type could have done it, but what would be the likelihood?"

"As I say, it's rare in whites, and even more so in other races. Only two percent of Hispanics and Negroes have it, and less than one percent of Orientals. No, I believe a match with Pollock would be pretty strong evidence."

Nita's years of experience told her that the most obvious explanation isn't always the right one. Skepticism was especially important in murder investigations. As she and Abel walked down the hall to where Finch was waiting, she reminded the doctor that Ruth's account would be crucial.

"Pollock obviously had the opportunity," she said,

"and he was strong enough to have done the deed, but what would his motive have been? That's why we need Ruth's memory to return, the sooner the better. If Pollock did it, only she can tell us why."

"And if he didn't," reasoned Abel, "only she is likely to know who did."

TWENTY-NINE.

Riding back to East Hampton in Finch's patrol car, Nita expressed her frustration at the lack of results from her questioning.

"I couldn't get anything out of her. Not only is she doped up, but she also has amnesia, at least about the crucial time just before the accident. Dr. Abel says we have to be patient, and really there's nothing more to be done with her until her condition improves, but we're losing valuable time. Meanwhile we'll just have to work some other angles."

"How can you do that without arousing suspicion?" asked Finch. "If you start questioning other people, word will soon be out that Metzger's death wasn't an accident."

"I think I can be more indirect than that," she said. "For instance, I could simply observe some of the likely suspects, see if I can detect the kinds of injuries Metzger's fingernails would have inflicted on their faces, arms, or hands."

Just then they passed The Creeks, and she gave him an example. "Starting with Ossorio. Fitz and I have a theory about him—nothing concrete, but it bears checking out. When we get back to the Sea Spray I think I'll phone The Creeks and see if I can pay him a visit."

"I'll drop you off at the inn, then stop by the cottage, see if the guys are around," said Finch. He had taken quite a liking to both Fitz and TJ, she noted with pleasure.

"Won't Harry—the chief, I mean—be expecting you back soon?" she asked, not wanting to get him in Dutch with his boss.

"They'd radio if I was needed," he replied, "so I'll take lunch now. I can swing by the dairy and pick up some sandwiches." He made a left off the highway onto Toilsome Lane, which curved right and became Gingerbread Lane just before it would have hit the railroad tracks. At the intersection with Race Lane, Tillinghast Dairy provided simple lunches for the local workmen. Nita waited in the car while Finch went in and placed his order.

"I hope egg salad is okay for everybody," he said as he returned to the car with four sandwiches in a paper bag. Nita offered to pay, but he insisted on treating. "Dairy products, eggs, bread, that's all they got here. Oh, and coffee, but I don't recommend it this late in the day. Been on the stove since five a.m. Your spoon'd stand up in it by now."

"We've got milk and root beer in the icebox at the cottage," Nita told him. "Some fruit as well. Unfortunately the donuts are all gone."

"Not surprised," said Finch with a chuckle. "Good thing, too." He patted his ample midsection as he headed out of Tillinghast's parking lot and back to the highway.

When they reached the Sea Spray, Nita said she'd go with him to the cottage first, in case the guys were still on the beach. But they had returned, and were rinsing off the salt and sand in the outdoor shower, splashing each other playfully and shaking the water out of their hair like wet puppies. They waved as they saw Finch's car approaching.

"Havin' a fine, fun-lovin' boy like that brings out the kid in you," he observed. "Me and my dad used to be the same way when I was that age, just a couple o' pals." Nita sensed some twenty-five years momentarily fall away as he looked back on happy memories.

"Well, let's make sure this boy of mine doesn't starve to death," she said, "or I'll never be an *abuela*—that's Spanish for grandma." He returned her smile, handed her the sandwiches, and went around the car to open the door for her. They walked to the cottage together as Fitz and TJ finished toweling off and slipped into their robes.

Nita waved the sandwich bag. "Hi, fellas. Look what Officer Finch has brought—lunch!" The news was received with enthusiasm. "It's cooler outside. We can eat on the porch," she suggested, and they pulled up chairs while she went to the kitchen and returned with milk, soda, fruit, glasses, and napkins.

"You guys get started," she said. "I'm going over to the inn to see if I can reach Ossorio. I'll explain when I get back. Meanwhile Officer Finch will fill you in."

"I think it's time we got on a first-name basis, don't you?" said Finch. "After all, TJ gave me permission, so I'd like to return the favor. How about calling me Earl from now on?" TJ beamed, and Fitz said he reckoned that would be fine.

Nita excused herself and headed for Mr. Bayley's office, where she got the number for The Creeks from the local phone book, a puny runt of a thing compared to its Manhattan counterpart. The switchboard gave her an outside line, and she dialed EA4-1472. After a few rings, Ossorio answered. Nita was aware that his and hers were not the only ears pressed to a receiver.

"*Buenas tardes, Señor* Ossorio," she began, hoping that her use of his native tongue would help dispel any wariness on his part. "This is Juanita Diaz speaking. We met at the funeral parlor, when you and the Brookses went to see Dr. Cooper."

"Yes, I remember," he replied, a bit vaguely. "I beg your pardon, but I thought your name was Fitzgerald. Am I mistaken? If so, I apologize."

His politeness, coupled with his English accent, threatened to disarm Nita, who had forgotten that she'd been introduced as Mrs. Juanita Fitzgerald, with no mention of her being a policewoman, only as a witness to the accident. Momentarily at a loss, she quickly regrouped.

"Oh, no, you're not mistaken, sir. It's I who must apologize for the confusion. Diaz is my maiden name. I use it professionally."

"Are you an artist?" he asked. It was common for female artists to keep their birth names, and Ossorio knew several of them. Lee Krasner had done it after she married Jackson Pollock, and so had Charlotte Park, a.k.a. Mrs. James Brooks. Likewise Cile Downs, who was Mrs. Sheridan Lord in private life, and the much-married Grace Hartigan, who was currently between husbands.

"Nothing so creative, I'm afraid. I can explain, but I'd prefer to do it in person. Would you mind if I came to see you? That is, if you're not too busy with the arrangements." Pollock's funeral was scheduled for the next day.

Ossorio was graciousness itself. "Not at all, *Señorita* Diaz, yclept *Señora* Fitzgerald. And please bring your charming husband. Come for tea this afternoon at four, if that is convenient."

"May I bring my son as well? His name is Timothy Juan, TJ for short. He's eight. I think he would enjoy meeting you and seeing The Creeks. We've heard a lot about the place and how beautiful it is."

"By all means," he replied. "It will be my pleasure to give your whole family the grand tour." *Excellent*, thought Nita. *Now I can observe him informally, and he'll be off his guard.*

THIRTY.

"Who was that?" asked Ted as Alfonso replaced the receiver. He had come into the central hall—where the telephone sat on an elaborately carved Chinese rosewood table—from the kitchen, where he was preparing a large casserole for the several guests who would be staying with them for the funeral.

"Juanita Diaz Fitzgerald, the lovely lady I met at Yardley and Williams on Sunday. She and her husband and son witnessed the accident. Their car was heading down Fireplace Road as Jackson's was going up. They saw the whole thing. I invited them to tea this afternoon."

"Why did she call?" Ted wondered.

"I don't really know. She was a bit mysterious, said she'd tell me in person. They're from the city, out here on holiday. Perhaps she's just curious to know more about Jackson. We shall soon find out.

"What time are we expecting Charles and Frank?" he

asked. Two of Jackson's brothers were flying in, Frank from California and Charles from Michigan.

Like an efficient social secretary, Ted had made all the connections. The long-distance telephone lines had been busy for the past two days.

"They're going to stay in the city tonight with Jay and Alma, and come out on the train tomorrow morning. Alma isn't well, so Jay begged off. The Potters will put them up—Jeffrey will pick them up at the station. Sande and 'Loie are driving down from Connecticut today with the kids and mother Stella. They'll stay here with us tonight and tomorrow night, and go back on Thursday unless there's some reason for them to stay on."

Alfonso was sanguine about Lee's relations with the Pollock family.

"I doubt Lee will be wanting them to hang around. She and Stella have their differences, and she's suspicious of Sande's motives. According to her, he thinks he's entitled to some compensation for all the years he babysat Jackson. I daresay he is, but not by her lights. I think she's being unreasonable, but she's in no state to be reasoned with. She told me that Jackson's will leaves everything to her, nothing to any of the brothers. That was certainly her doing—she wants complete control of his estate, just as she had control of his career when he was alive. Even Sidney Janis, one of the shrewdest dealers in New York, has to get her consent before he makes a sale."

Ted sniffed his disapproval. "As if Sidney doesn't know

what he's doing. She has him to thank for Jackson's prices. Why, he told me Ben Heller is paying eight thousand dollars for a big 1950 canvas. Eight thousand, can you believe! Lee should be kissing Sidney's ring instead of second-guessing him."

"But you know," Alfonso reflected, "when Jackson boasted about his prices, his artist friends weren't pleased. In fact, to be blunt, they were envious. Even as they were slapping him on the back and toasting him with the drinks he bought them, you could almost hear them thinking, *Why him and not me?*"

Ted agreed. "The art world is so competitive, and such a slave to fashion. You're all the rage one season and passé the next. At least in the dance world you know where you stand. Either you can do it or you can't." His eyes dropped, and he shrugged. "Anyway, I'd better get back to work." He turned and headed for the kitchen.

Alfonso understood his sudden change of tone. Five years earlier, just as Ted's career with George Balanchine's New York City Ballet was shifting into high gear, he gave it up to move with Ossorio to The Creeks. Once it was decided they had never discussed it again, but they both knew what that sacrifice had entailed. When Ted closed the stage door, it was locked behind him. Now, at thirty-five, he was the male equivalent of a stay-at-home helpmeet, entirely dependent on Alfonso. But with that dependence came mutual devotion, as well as material comfort and travel.

A further benefit was a glittering social life among Alfonso's wide circle of friends that extended well beyond the art world's narrow confines, including the film and stage luminaries Ruth had touted to Edith, as well as intellectuals, scientists, and religious leaders. When guests crossed the threshold at The Creeks, it was Ted who orchestrated the occasion while staying largely in the background.

"Oh, they're not interested in me at all," he would confide to those few, like Jackson and Lee, who became his intimates. Then, with a mischievous grin and a wink, he'd add, "but when I make myself interesting, they change their minds," leaving it to his listener's imagination what "interesting" meant.

Now, in a chef's apron over shorts and a T-shirt, he busied himself with preparations for the onslaught of guests, both at The Creeks and at the funeral. After the service at the Springs Chapel and burial in Green River Cemetery, there would be a reception at the Pollock house. With no idea how many people might turn up, but anticipating a crowd, Lee had agreed to leave the catering in Ted's capable hands. He had ordered plenty of food from Dreesen's and liquor from Dakers' to be delivered to the house on Wednesday afternoon. He'd also called Vetault's to get some flowers for the chapel—nothing ostentatious, just a wreath of daisies like the ones in Jackson's garden.

But no matter how efficient he was, there was no way

to prepare adequately for the inevitable emotional strain, which he knew would only be increased by the presence of the other mourners. Somehow Lee had managed to erect a seemingly impenetrable barrier that walled in her feelings, but Ted was not so resolute. He didn't think he'd be up to the service or the interment, so he had volunteered to stay behind at Lee's house and prepare for the reception.

Better to grieve alone in private than to risk an embarrassing breakdown in front of witnesses. There'll be more than enough of that without me adding to it, he reasoned.

THIRTY-ONE.

Just shy of four o'clock, the Fitzgerald family pulled into the porte cochère at the entrance to the main house at The Creeks, a Mediterranean-style villa with a cool green tile roof and stucco walls painted a light beige to reflect the summer sun. To get there from the highway, they had driven down a half-mile private road that wound through landscaped grounds, past the carriage house-cum-garage and pergola, and around a circular drive enclosing a fountain surrounded by a lush rose garden, now past its best but still impressive.

"¡Hala!" exclaimed TJ with characteristic enthusiasm for all things new and different. "This is some place! You say only two guys live here? I bet they have a whole bunch of servants to take care of it, like those fancy houses in the movies."

"Let's go in and find out," said his father as Ossorio came to the door to greet them. Nita introduced him to her son, whose hand he shook with courtly formality. She noted that his arms, revealed by his short-sleeved sports shirt, showed no evidence of wounds made by a woman's fingernails. Nor did his face.

"Welcome to all three Fitzgeralds," he said with a smile. "You may leave the car right there. We're not expecting anyone else until later. Some of Jackson's family will be here this evening." He ushered the trio inside.

The entrance foyer led up three steps to a two-story hallway that spanned the living and dining rooms. Glass doors opened onto a brick-paved terrace overlooking Georgica Pond, providing cross ventilation and a spectacular view across the pond to the ocean beach. With a gentle breeze activating bamboo wind chimes hung in the open doorways, and the afternoon sun sparkling on the placid water, the arrangement conjured the world of genteel summertime leisure and pleasure for which the estate had been designed.

Knowing that the Herters intended to use it only as a seasonal residence, the architect, Grosvenor Atterbury, had capitalized on the site's proximity to the ocean. Within a symmetrical plan, he placed the living room, dining room, and bedrooms in matching wings on the house's south side to take maximum advantage of the view, with the service areas, the music room, and the couple's art studios on the north side, where indirect sunlight was most advantageous. Since everything would be shut down by October and not reopened until May or

June, there was no need for storm windows or an extensive heating system.

At first the lack of winterization was a challenge for Alfonso and Ted, who planned on living at The Creeks full-time. In heavy sweaters and long underwear during the day, and under an eiderdown comforter at night, they shivered through the winter of 1952, their first year in residence. By closing off the upstairs rooms they were able to maximize what heat there was, and the southern exposure helped warm the downstairs on sunny days.

Gradually they had renovated and insulated to the point where the building was now a cozy year-round home. There was enough space for Alfonso to indulge his penchant for collecting eclectic furniture, exotic artifacts, and modern art—even for him to house the collection of "raw art" by the self-taught and the insane assembled by his friend, the French painter Jean Dubuffet, whose plans for an Art Brut museum in Paris had fallen through. And the spacious barnlike main studio, custom built for Albert Herter, was a great improvement on Alfonso's small loft in the MacDougal Alley carriage house where he and Ted had lived before moving to The Creeks.

"Please wait here a moment while I ask Ted to put the kettle on," said Alfonso. "He'll make some iced tea while I show you around, then we can all have refreshments on the terrace." Raising his eyebrows, he turned to Nita. "And you can tell me to what I owe the pleasure of your visit."

As soon as he was gone, TJ tugged at his father's shirtsleeve. "Hey, Dad, look at that!" He pointed to a grimacing African mask staring down menacingly from the wall above them. It reminded Fitz of the mask that had covered the face of Wifredo Lam as he lay dead on the floor of his Greenwich Village studio thirteen years earlier. In spite of himself, it gave him the shivers, though he didn't let on to TJ.

"If you wanted to scare away the Fuller Brush man, that would be your guy," he joked. "I'm glad he's up there and we're down here. I hope he's nailed to the wall." He glanced at Nita, who was also remembering the photographs of Lam's body in its "exquisite corpse" costume.

"I see you've met Caddington," said Ossorio, returning from the kitchen. "I found him at the Marché aux Puces in Paris. He belongs to the Yoruba tribe, so I'm told. He bears a striking resemblance to the headmaster at St. Richard's School, where I spent my formative years." He let them guess at the memories that led him to name the fearsome mask after his former boarding school teacher.

More wonders awaited them in the adjoining rooms, including several African sculptures, intriguing fossils, a rock crystal on a wooden stand, a large decorated whale tooth that Ossorio told them was called scrimshaw, and a shrunken head from Ecuador that TJ silently coveted.

On the walls were abstract canvases by contemporary artists, including Ossorio himself, and a large one by Pollock—roughly seven feet tall and ten feet wide—that took pride of place in the main salon. The room was sparsely furnished, just a settee and two chairs clustered around a magnificent Persian carpet in front of the fireplace, nothing to block the view of the painting. Ossorio told them it was called simply *Number 1, 1950.* Pollock didn't like to title his paintings.

"I have several of Jackson's pictures," he said, "but this is the largest. I bought it from his one-man show the year it was painted—he was in top form then. That show was full of masterpieces. I fell in love with it as soon as I saw it, but it was too big for the place where Ted and I were living, so I had to wait until we moved here before I could claim it from the gallery. Jackson was thrilled to see it on this wall, with the gorgeous reflected light from the pond dancing on it." He motioned for them to step closer to get the full effect.

Not sure of what their reaction should be, and with no title to give them a hint, Nita and Fitz limited themselves to noncommittal murmurs, but TJ felt no such constraint.

"What's it supposed to be?" he asked.

Instead of dismissing the youngster's frank curiosity, as most sophisticated adults would have done, Ossorio answered him respectfully.

"That is an excellent question, *Señor* TJ, one that Jackson and I often discussed. For both of us, art is a form of visual communication, but while I tend to use figures and symbols that people might recognize, in paintings like this one Jackson went beyond such devices. He opened up a new world of imagination, one that doesn't depend on familiar landmarks."

He stood about six feet back from the painting and beckoned TJ to join him.

"When you stand here," he pointed out, "your side vision doesn't quite extend all the way across the canvas, so the painting draws you in." Together they studied it in silence for a few moments, while Fitz and Nita were impressed by Ossorio's solicitude.

"Jackson once told me," continued Ossorio, "that people should look at abstract art the way they listen to music. Just enjoy it for what it is without worrying about what it means. But that's not to say it has no meaning at all. It really depends on you. What do you think?"

"Golly," replied TJ, "I'm not sure. The colors are pretty, and I like the way they sorta float on the surface. And it's all splotchy, like rain on the window." He turned to look up at Ossorio, who nodded his agreement.

"Yes, I see what you mean," he said.

Encouraged, TJ continued, "So if I think it looks like a rainy day, that's okay?"

"Certainly," said Ossorio. "You're using your imagination, giving it your own meaning. That's the important thing. But let's go closer and I'll show you something interesting."

As they approached the painting, Ossorio lifted TJ up to his shoulder so his head was level with the top of the canvas. "Look at the top right corner," he prompted, "and tell me what you see."

"Oh, *mira eso*, it's a hand!" TJ exclaimed, "and there's another one!" He pointed to the left. "A whole row of them!"

"*Sí, Señor* TJ. You can find lots of handprints once you know what to look for. Why do you think Jackson put them there?"

"Did he do it on purpose?" asked TJ.

Ossorio lowered the boy to the floor and crouched down beside him. "Oh, yes. It's a kind of signature, much more personal than the written one." He pointed out Pollock's name and the number 50, the year it was painted, along the bottom edge at the left. "Everything Jackson did on canvas was deliberate. He said there were no accidents, however spontaneous his technique. He had remarkable, almost uncanny control of the liquid paint he used—ordinary house paint, but what extraordinary results he got with it. I can only aspire to his level of intuitive creativity. Perhaps I'll get there some day, but I have a long way to go."

THIRTY-TWO.

"Well, we don't have far to go for our tea," interjected Ted as he joined them. Pushing a rolling cart bearing a pitcher of iced tea with lemons, a plate of home-baked scones, and ramekins of jam and butter, he waved them outside to the terrace, where a glass-topped wrought-iron table and matching chairs with cushioned seats were waiting under the shade of a large canvas umbrella.

"I'm Ted," he informed them as he unloaded the cart, "the hostess with the mostes' on the ball," quoting Ethel Merman. "And you are the Fitzgeralds. Delighted to meet you." He bowed deeply and straightened to display a charming dimpled smile.

"I'm Fitz, this is Nita, and our son TJ." Hands were shaken all around. "It was good of you to go to all this trouble, especially since you have to get ready for the funeral tomorrow."

"Absolutely no trouble at all," Ted assured him. "We

have tea on the terrace every afternoon. It's lovely that you could join us." His expertise at making guests feel welcome was well practiced.

"Oh, dear," remarked Nita as he handed around the glasses, "you've got some nasty scratches on your arm. Shouldn't you put something on them?" She had spotted what looked like claw marks on his left forearm.

Ted shrugged off her concern, which—though he didn't realize it—was strictly professional. "It's nothing, really. I was trying to make some headway, forgive the pun, in the rose beds. So many dead heads to clip, so few hours in the day. The thorns are such a menace—I really must get gloves with longer gauntlets."

"I'm seriously thinking of having all those bushes pulled up," said Ossorio. "They were planted by the Herters, and they were only here in summer. Flower gardens are too seasonal—they look awful in winter, dead and depressing. Evergreens would be much more suitable for a year-round garden. And a lot less work for our gardener."

"Meaning me," said Ted with a chuckle. "I'm Mr. Fixit as well. Alfonso doesn't know how to change a lightbulb. The only place where he can manage on his own is in the studio."

"Don't you have a staff?" asked Fitz. "Surely you can't run this big estate without servants."

"But we do, almost entirely alone, that is. The cleaning lady comes in once a week, and she helps clear up after a party, but that's it. I'm teasing about Alfonso, he does his fair share around the house, but he really is worse than useless in the garden. He only has to approach a flower or a shrub to kill it, and God help the rhododendrons if he ever decides to take up pruning."

Ossorio expressed deep resentment at this offense to his horticultural prowess, and the two began to banter back and forth, much to the amusement of their guests. Presently Ted excused himself, pleading the demands of a *boeuf bourguignon* in progress.

"Want to see what I've got cooking?" he asked TJ, who said sure, and off they went to the kitchen, at which point Ossorio decided it was time to find out the reason for Nita's call.

Having earlier considered Ossorio to be a prime suspect, she was now having second thoughts. His face and arms were unmarked. The scratches on Ted's left arm might have been made by rose thorns, or maybe by fingernails— it would take a closer examination to find out for sure. If they were human inflicted, and a blood test matched the tissue samples, it would be damning evidence. Perhaps it was he who tried to head off Pollock, Kligman, and Metzger on their way into the concert.

She glanced at Fitz, but he was deliberately focusing on the view, leaving her to improvise.

"I told you I use my maiden name professionally," she began, "but I didn't say what that profession is. I'm a New York City police detective."

Ossorio couldn't have been more stunned. "Detective

Juanita Diaz? You astonish me. But then I imagine you astonish most people, including your handsome husband." He beamed indulgently on the couple, earning a nod of agreement from a blushing Fitz and once again disarming Nita. *This fellow could charm the birds out of the trees*, she said to herself. I mustn't let myself be taken in.

"Fitz, TJ, and I are out here on vacation," she explained, "and we just happened to be there when the car accident happened. As you know, Ruth Kligman is in the hospital. She was incoherent when I gave her first aid at the scene, and she's been in and out of consciousness ever since. The chief of the East Hampton Town police asked me, as a favor, to question her when she came to, but she seems to have lost her memory of the events leading up to the crash. I was hoping you might be able to fill some of the gaps."

"What do you mean? What sort of gaps?"

"Well, for instance, how far did Pollock get that night? Did he make it as far as The Creeks?" She knew this was a loaded question, since Ossorio had told Dr. Cooper that Pollock and the women didn't attend the concert.

Ossorio answered without hesitation. "If he did get this far, I never saw him. The concert began a little after nine. I introduced the pianist and the chamber orchestra, then sat down to enjoy the program. The gates were open, so he could have driven in, changed his mind, and driven out again. Since he was late, perhaps he decided not to interrupt."

From their tour of the ground floor, Nita remembered that the music room's west windows faced the circular drive. "Wouldn't his lights have been visible from inside?" she asked. "Surely that would have been noticed."

"You're very observant, but of course you're a detective, so I shouldn't be surprised. However, the driveway was lined with parked cars—we had more than fifty people here—so the windows would have been shielded. I'm sure a car could have driven around the circle without attracting attention."

So someone outside could have encountered Pollock and the girls without anyone inside seeing them, thought Nita. *And the music would have drowned out an argument several yards away. But is that what happened? Was someone outside—Ted, perhaps?*

With some fifty witnesses it shouldn't be hard to verify that Ossorio was in the music room during the concert, or if he was absent for any part of the time. But what about Ted? Nita decided to pursue that question indirectly.

"Do you think Ted might have seen them? Or was he in the music room, too?"

"No, I believe he was in the dining room, laying out the food and drinks for the reception, or in the kitchen. Either way I doubt he'd notice a latecoming car, and after what happened I think he would have mentioned it. But why don't you ask him?" Ossorio rose and directed them toward the kitchen. "Besides, it's time to rescue TJ. Ted has probably put him to work."

Sure enough, Fitz and Nita found their son standing

on a stepstool at the long central worktable. Clad in an apron, coated in a dusting of flour, and elbow deep in a huge bowl of bread dough, he was kneading away fiercely as Ted urged him on. His efforts, punctuated by loud huffing and grunting, were receiving enthusiastic approval.

"That's right, sock it in the gut! Punch it in the ribs! Give it the old one-two! The harder you hit it, the better it tastes."

Fitz exchanged amused looks with Nita. "You two are having entirely too much fun," he said to Ted, then addressed his son. "If you're finished punishing that dough, it's time we were going. Your mom wants a word with Ted, so if Alfonso will show me where the washroom is I'll get you cleaned up."

The baker's apprentice turned to his mentor for guidance. "Am I finished? Did I punch it hard enough?"

"You beat the stuffing out of it," Ted told him. "But it will rise again like magic. I'll get four big loaves out of this batch. If you promise to come back, I'll save one of them for you."

"Will you really? *¡Qué bueno!* Can we, Mom? Can we, Dad?"

With assurance that they would return in a couple of days, after the funeral guests had left, TJ agreed to be relieved of kitchen duty and headed off to the washroom. This gave Nita the chance to question Ted tactfully, without putting him on guard.

"I'm sure you're wondering why I asked to come over,"

she began, then explained her mission as she had to Ossorio. She got an even more animated reaction from Ted.

"A detective? Well, strike me pink! Apparently the plainclothes branch is launching a charm offensive." Another dimpled grin spread into a wicked smile. "I must ask Fitz to rate your undercover work."

"Making suggestive remarks to a police detective is a criminal offense," she countered. "Perhaps I should run you in. I'm sure I have my handcuffs here somewhere." She pretended to search for them in her handbag while Ted pretended to be contrite.

"Seriously," she said, "I do want to ask you something, on behalf of Chief Steele. He's trying to trace Pollock's movements on Saturday night. Is there any chance he and the girls actually got here, but decided not to stay?"

Ted's brow furrowed thoughtfully. "I suppose it's possible, but I'm sure they didn't come into the house, or I would have noticed them. I was shuttling between the kitchen and the dining room, getting ready for the reception."

"You didn't hear a car drive in late, by any chance?" She was gauging his responses carefully, looking for any hesitation or uneasiness, but he was apparently untroubled by her probing.

"No, I didn't, but the music was loud enough that I doubt I would have heard a car, unless it pulled right under the porte cochere. Maybe not even then, if I was in the dining room."

Now Ted began to wonder where this was leading. "But let me ask you a question. Why does it matter if they got here or not? Jackson did say they'd be at the concert, but we know they weren't. Maybe the girls convinced him to go somewhere else. Maybe he took them out for drinks, or to the movies."

Easy does it, thought Nita, *don't make him think he's under suspicion. But it does sound like he's trying to deflect any hint that they could have turned up here.*

"I believe Chief Steele is investigating those possibilities," she hedged. "He just wants to cover all the bases, and he's shorthanded so he asked me to cover this one, just as a favor, you understand. Nothing official, I'm strictly off duty."

"If Harry Steele has any sense," said Ted with conviction, "he'll recruit you. The East Hampton Town force is extremely short on glamour, not to mention brains. And you've got both."

THIRTY-THREE.

Wednesday, August 15

Lee spent the morning on the phone, relentlessly badgering everyone involved in the funeral. Unable to persuade Clement Greenberg, the art critic whose enthusiasm had helped launch Pollock's career, to deliver the eulogy, she turned to Fred Williams for help. He lined up the pastor from the Amagansett Presbyterian Church, a house of worship in which the artist had never set foot. Although they came from Presbyterian stock, LeRoy and Stella Pollock disdained the church and had not had their sons baptized.

When Lee announced that the funeral would be held in the chapel, Jackson's brothers were surprised and somewhat offended. Was she doing it on purpose, to spite them? With that possibility in mind, Sande had questioned her choice of venue.

"Wouldn't the funeral parlor be more appropriate?" Sande had asked.

Lee was emphatic. "No. When I went over there to discuss the arrangements, it was obvious that their rooms are way too small. I'm sure you realize that this will not be a strictly family and friends affair. It's going to be a mob scene, Sande, so I had to keep that in mind. Besides, the chapel is much closer to the cemetery. My decision was simply practical."

It was also final, no arguments. The matter was settled, with the implicit understanding that the family could like it or lump it.

In fact Lee was right about practicality. For the past two days, every time she replaced the receiver the phone would ring with a call from yet another artist, critic, curator, dealer, or collector telling her that he or she would be attending. Many of them were already in residence nearby for the summer, and others would be coming out from the city by car or train. Springs was not much more than a hundred miles from the center of the art universe. And in spite of her attitude toward the Bonackers, she knew she couldn't prevent a contingent of them from turning up to say farewell to their drinking buddy.

She was having less success with the people she wanted to be there. In addition to Greenberg, who turned her down flat with the excuse that he couldn't praise a man who had killed his passenger, her attorney, Gerry Weinstock, also begged off.

"I'm sorry, Lee, I have to be in court on Wednesday. But Mags and the kids are there, so they'll be at the funeral. I'll be out at the weekend, and we can go over the will and anything else you need to review then. Right now you have to think about protecting Jackson's paintings in the studio. Put a padlock on it immediately, and for God's sake keep it locked during the reception." The wisdom of that advice was obvious.

Her biggest disappointment was her brother, Irving, who also pleaded the pressure of work. With several of the staff at his insurance company out on vacation, he explained, his boss couldn't spare him.

"But I need you, Izzy," she insisted, using his childhood nickname to underscore their blood tie. "I'm going to be surrounded by Jackson's family—I need someone in my corner!"

"Come on, Lee," he said, "you'll have plenty of friends around, you don't need me." He pointed out that their sister Udel would be there with her husband and kids, so she wouldn't be the only Krasner in the room.

"Don't give me that, Izzy," she retorted. "They'll be completely useless. They have no idea how to behave with these people. The sharks are already circling, waiting for a chance to take a bite out of Jackson's estate. If they can't profit from his death, they'll try to undermine his reputation out of spite. You know how to stand up to them. You know what's at stake."

He knew, all right. It was Irving who had persuaded Lee to insure the contents of the studio for the full market value after Jackson installed a Salamander kerosene stove to heat the building. Terrified that he would spill the fuel and carelessly drop a lighted match or cigarette into it, she had asked her brother to write a policy that would protect her inheritance in case a fire destroyed the many canvases and works on paper lining the walls, in the flat file, and in the storage racks. Lee was his only heir.

With the value of his work increasing annually, thanks to Sidney Janis's expert promotion, the inventory represented financial security for Lee in the event of Jackson's death. Since she had stifled her own career to promote his, there was virtually no market for her work. She knew it would take years to establish one, if ever.

Most dealers, even the women, scorned female artists, believing them to be bad risks. Whether justified or not, this prejudice prevented many deserving women from achieving the kind of success—both critical and financial—enjoyed by their male colleagues, who often reinforced that attitude.

Even Jackson, who had persuaded his dealer to give Lee a solo show and often expressed pride in her accomplishments, was not above taking a cheap shot at her in private.

"She's talented, plenty," he once told a friend, "but great art needs a pecker. Not even Lee's got that."

Perhaps to compensate for that physical deficit, she had developed some metaphorical alternatives: an exceptionally stiff backbone, a very hard head, and plenty of guts.

THIRTY-FOUR.

"What are you going to wear?" asked Fitz as he watched Nita rummaging through the closet. He had laid out the white long-sleeved shirt, striped necktie, sports jacket, and navy blue trousers he had packed for evenings out; although, until now, with everything here so informal, he'd had no occasion to wear them.

Sighing with frustration, Nita examined and rejected item after item of clothing.

"Everything I have is too, I don't know, too cheerful," she said. "Maybe I should run down to that little department store in town and buy something black, or at least a dark color." The various church funerals she had attended in Spanish Harlem led her to expect heavy solemnity and acres of mourning clothes, especially on the women.

"Maybe you should ask Ossorio," he suggested. "He'll know what's appropriate." That seemed like a good idea to Nita, so she walked over to the inn and used the office phone.

Ossorio told her that Fitz could forget the jacket and tie, and that her summer clothing would be fine. No one was going to dress in black, and no head covering was required for the women. The service would be brief and informal, without organ music or hymns.

"Nothing like the Roman Catholic funerals you and I are used to," he explained. "Lee tells me that the casket will be closed, so there will be no viewing, no parade of mourners. The minister will say a few words, perhaps one or two others will speak, then the hearse will take the body to Green River for burial. I expect that's where the real grieving will take place. Then a lot of people will go back to the house, where crocodile tears will flow as freely as the whisky."

"My goodness, you are a cynic. Surely his close friends and family are sincere."

"Even they are ambivalent. I don't mean his mother—she's heartbroken, though she won't show it in public. I went to her room to check on her last night, and I found her sitting in a chair, sobbing. When I tried to comfort her, she pulled herself together and I knew she'd not break down again. Like his brothers, she realized Jackson was more or less living on borrowed time. She tried to look the other way when he went off the rails, but she's no fool.

"Still, in spite of the heartache he caused her, Stella is enormously proud of Jackson. Even though she's just a simple countrywoman, she understands the importance of what he achieved. After she composed herself, she looked me straight in the eye and said, 'His work is done.'"

"I don't think Fitz and I should go to the house," said Nita. "We just want to pay our respects." They had not been in contact with Lee, and didn't want to intrude. Their real reason for attending the funeral was to see if anyone might qualify as a suspect in Metzger's murder—someone with a face wound, or with scratches like Ted's on his arm.

"Earl Finch, the police officer who supervised the accident scene, has offered to let TJ stay at his house during the service. He lives nearby, so we can drop him off and pick him up afterward. How long do you think it will be?"

"At the chapel? Half an hour at most. Another hour if you go to the cemetery. There will be plenty of cars, so it will take them a while to get there, even though it's only a mile or so away. Then I'm sure several people will want to say something at the graveside. By six o'clock everyone will be hungry. And thirsty." Anticipating as many gate-crashers as invited guests, he and Ted had laid on plenty of refreshments, solid and liquid.

Ossorio knew what to expect. "Many sorrows—some real, some feigned—will be drowned tonight. Lee's antennae will detect the difference."

Armed with directions to the Finch residence—north on Fireplace, left on Gardiner, third on the left, look for the yellow mailbox—the Fitzgeralds headed out.

"Earl says he's got chickens in his yard," TJ informed his parents, "and a dog I can play with." The only chickens he had ever seen up close were lying dead in the butcher shop window. And as much as he would have liked a dog of his own, pets were not allowed in their Stuyvesant Town apartment.

Finch's wife, Grace, greeted them as they parked in the driveway.

"Glad to know you, Nita, Fitz, TJ. I have to apologize for Earl. He's on duty today—you'll see him at the funeral, but in an official capacity. They're expecting quite a crowd, so he has to direct traffic."

Sensing TJ's disappointment, Grace added, "But he'll come home as soon as the service is over. You folks'll stay for dinner, I hope." They accepted the invitation gratefully.

"Meanwhile," she continued, "I've got some fresh-baked cookies in the kitchen." She addressed TJ. "How about you tuck into 'em, and then I'll introduce you to Sally and her pups."

TJ's jaw dropped. "You've got puppies?" he cried. "¡Qué maravilloso!"

Nita explained that her son spoke playground Spanish, especially when he got excited. "Maybe the puppies first," she suggested, "then the cookies."

"Okay, off we go," Grace said, and led TJ to the backyard, where a kennel held the Finches' yellow Labrador bitch and her four offspring.

Fitz and Nita waved goodbye and headed back to the car. "I wonder if we'll be able to get him to leave," said Fitz. "The Finches may just have to adopt him."

The service was not due to start for a quarter of an hour, but already the chapel's small parking lot was overflowing, and cars were parked at Ashawagh Hall and along Amagansett Road and Fireplace Road. Finch spotted their Chevy and moved aside a sawhorse barrier so they could park in the reserved section.

"We dropped TJ off at your place," Fitz told him. "Thanks to Grace for looking after him, and for the invitation to dinner."

"Happy to have you," said Finch. "Maybe you'll have some more ideas about the Metzger business by the time we sit down tonight."

"I hope so," said Nita. "I called the hospital this morning, and Kligman's memory hasn't improved. Until it comes back, we're kind of grasping at straws."

"How about the lab report on the skin fragments?"

"They're still waiting for that, too. It can take up to a week."

THIRTY-FIVE.

People later remarked that the day of the funeral was incongruously beautiful for such a sad occasion—one friend of the family called it a day for swimming and beach umbrellas, not for mourning. Even with the doors and windows open and a couple of large ceiling fans running on high, the chapel was oppressively hot.

By the time Fitz and Nita squeezed in to stand at the back, there must have been a hundred people already in attendance. The children were fidgety, and the adults who had neglected to bring paper fans were using whatever they could find, including notices pulled off the bulletin board.

The men wisely wore short-sleeved sports shirts and T-shirts, and Nita was relieved to see that the women were in summer clothing—cotton dresses or skirts, even a few in slacks, with sleeveless blouses or halter tops, none of them somber. The only exception was the elderly woman in the first pew on the right. They assumed she was Jackson's mother, Stella, whose midnight-blue dress had doubtless seen other funerals. Flanked by three of her four surviving sons, she sat in silence as even more people tried to force their way inside and many others peered in through the open windows.

Nita and Fitz recognized several of the people in attendance. In the row behind the Pollocks sat Alfonso with Jim, Charlotte, and Cile. Beside Cile was a tall man they guessed was her husband. Across the narrow aisle they spotted Tom Collins with his wife and son Mike, and Dan Miller with his family. Pete and Nina Federico from Jungle Pete's were also there.

Soberly dressed in a gray blouse and navy blue skirt, a solitary woman sat in the front left pew. Nita realized that she must be the deceased's wife, Lee Krasner. *Odd,* Nita thought, *why is she all on her own? If, God forbid, it were me at my husband's funeral, I'd want my family beside me.*

Lee's tactic was carefully calculated to insulate herself as much as possible. Her sister, brother-in-law, and their children were seated behind her instead of at her side. She was determined not to show any emotion, but in case her lips trembled or a tear escaped, her face would not be visible to the crowd and neither her family nor Jackson's would see.

She had chosen an expensive walnut casket. No one would be able to criticize her for skimping on Jackson's send-off. Thank goodness Alfonso had offered to pay for it—she'd returned from Europe to find a mere $350 in their bank account. Of course she intended to pay him back, once the will was probated and she could start earning money from Jackson's estate. But that would take a while, and she was wondering how she'd manage in the meantime.

Maybe Irving would tide her over. He knew how much the estate was worth. The larger paintings were selling for thousands, and he had written the policy that covered them. If he could just help her get through the next few months, she would return his money with interest.

Having delayed the service while the chapel filled to overflowing, at four forty-five Reverend George Nicholson stepped to the lectern beside the casket. The chatter in the room subsided.

Never having met the deceased, the pastor was forced to rely on platitudes.

"We are gathered here today to bid farewell to our neighbor Jackson. I am told he was a good man; a loving husband to Lee; a son who revered his mother, Stella; a proud brother of Charles, Jay, Frank, and Sanford; kind and generous to his many friends; and a great artist. As we commit his body to eternal rest, his spirit shall live on in his paintings and shall find everlasting life with Christ."

Lee had let it be known that Nicholson would be the only one to speak—no spontaneous words from the floor would be permitted. Anyone with something to say could wait until they got to the cemetery. Frankly, given the heat and the crowd, everyone was relieved by that decision, yet many found it strange that Lee had chosen a clergyman to deliver the eulogy.

Wasn't Jackson an atheist? Or at least a nonbeliever? "Fuck all the God shit," that's what he'd said more than once. "Leave that to the Salvation Army." How ironic that a man of God was about to close the book on him.

The pastor opened the book and read from the New Testament, Romans 8—a singularly unfortunate choice of scripture.

There is therefore now no condemnation to them which are in Christ Jesus, who walk not after the flesh, but after the Spirit. For the law of the Spirit of life in Christ Jesus has made me free from the law of sin and death.

For what the law could not do, in that it was weak through the flesh, God sending his own Son in the likeness of sinful flesh, and for sin, condemned sin in the flesh: That the righteousness of the law might be fulfilled in us, who walk not after the flesh, but after the Spirit.

For they that are after the flesh do mind the things of the flesh; but they that are after the Spirit the things of the Spirit. For to be carnally minded is death; but to be spiritually minded is life and peace.

He closed the book to a stunned silence. Not a single amen followed the reading.

Reverend Nicholson punted. "Let us pray."

Many voices, some full-throated, others muted, joined his as he intoned the Lord's Prayer. Fitz and Nita, both lapsed Catholics, recited the prayer quietly. Even those who did not speak bowed their heads. This time there was a chorus of amens at the end, and several people crossed themselves.

Lee stood, marched down the aisle and out to where the hearse was waiting. She had remained dry-eyed and outwardly calm, even as stomach acid flooded her throat and her bowels churned. She'd been afraid her chronic colitis would act up, and sure enough it had, brought on by Nicholson's embarrassing eulogy. What an idiot she had been to imagine that a minister would be the right choice. How could he go on about sinful flesh, when that was what got Jackson and that other little tramp killed? Christ Jesus, indeed! It would have served him right if Jackson had jumped up out of the coffin and decked him.

People began to file out past Nita and Fitz, who were unobtrusively checking the men for telltale wounds. None were apparent, so they went outside to mingle with the crowd and see if they could spot anything on those who had watched through the windows. Only the Pollock family and Jim Brooks stayed behind. As he and Jackson's brothers carried the casket to the hearse, Stella thanked the pastor for his comforting words, respectfully suspending her antipathy to organized religion and politely ignoring his biblical faux pas.

The group gathered outside felt no such compunctions.

"Carnally minded is right," snorted Cile's husband, Sheridan. "Screwing Ruth is all Jackson thought about, and talked about, for the past five months. Couldn't get enough of her, or so he said. Wishful thinking is my guess. Just like his painting lately—all talk, no action." There were murmurs of agreement, especially from the women, while some of the men were more willing to give Pollock the benefit of the doubt.

Paul Brach, one of the younger artists who hung around him, genuinely looking up to him but also hoping to absorb some of his luster, upheld the majority opinion.

"I'm inclined to agree with Sherry. He loved to brag, but when it came right down to it, I think it was bull-shit. Were any of you at the Cedar Bar in January when we turned the tables on him?" Apparently no one in the group had been, giving Brach the green light to tell a story he relished.

"A few of the boys were getting sick of him coming on to our wives and girlfriends, slobbering all over them and propositioning them, just to make us jealous and pro-voke a scene. He was good at that, loved to watch the girls squirm and the guys fume, maybe even take a slug at him. That was his idea of fun.

"So we chipped in and hired a prostitute—a nice-looking call girl, not a streetwalker. We told her what to expect, and how to react. We escorted her in, sat her down, bought her a drink, and acted like she was a new girlfriend. Sure enough, Jack takes the bait. He starts sweet-talking her and insulting us, calls us a bunch of fucking ass-kissers and second-rate followers of Jackson Pollock, the great genius in the studio and in bed. He says, come over to the Earle with me, honey, and I'll show you why they all envy me.

"We'd heard this line before, and it didn't work on our real dates—as he knew it wouldn't. But to his amazement, she says okay, I'll get my coat. The look on Jack's face was priceless. He mumbles something about having to go to the john and disappears. Poof, gone, just like that, apparently out through the kitchen. The whole table is in stitches."

The following week, much to everyone's surprise, Pollock was back at the Cedar, carrying on as if nothing humiliating had happened to him. Brach surmised that, in the time-honored way of drunks, he had actually forgotten the incident. But the patrons of the bar had not, and there were snickers and snide remarks behind Pollock's back—that is, until he latched onto Ruth, or rather she attached herself to him. Then the young bucks wanted to hit on *his* date.

THIRTY-SIX.

"That was quite a performance," said Fitz as he and Earl, each working on a can of Schlitz, sat at the Finches' kitchen table while the women busied themselves preparing dinner. Grace had laid on a mess of bluefish, nicely scaled and gutted, which they were stuffing with breadcrumbs, onions, and fresh herbs from the garden.

"I couldn't hear what the reverend said, but I got an earful from the folks comin' out," Earl told him. "The ones who weren't laughin' their heads off were shakin' 'em in disbelief. What did he say that got everybody so riled up?"

Fitz gave him a summary. "He read from scripture about sinful flesh, a topic I'm sure Mrs. Pollock didn't want raised under the circumstances. No doubt he didn't mean to, but he rubbed her nose in it."

Just then TJ appeared in the doorway, with Sally at his heels. They both were peppered with twigs and leaves, and were panting in unison.

"*¡Mira lo que encontré!*" TJ shouted, then apologized to his non-Spanish-speaking hosts. "Oh, sorry, I mean look what I found." He held out his hand to Fitz and opened it to reveal a necklace of blue glass beads.

"Where did you get this?" his father asked.

"I found it in the woods. Grace said I could take Sally for a walk, but to stay off the road, so we went out behind the house. There are trails back there—it's really neat. Grace said we wouldn't get lost 'cause Sally knows her way home, so I just followed her. Pretty soon we got to a road and I started to turn back, but then I recognized it. It was where the accident happened—you can still see the skid marks. And a couple of little trees are all bent and broken where the car ran over them."

He stopped to catch his breath, and to see if his parents would disapprove of his returning to the scene, but they simply waited for him to continue. He couldn't have known that his ramble would take him to Fireplace Road.

"Sally was rooting around in the leaves, so I went over to look at what she was digging for and I found the necklace. I guess maybe it came off the dead lady that was under the car."

Fitz beamed at his son. "I think he has the makings of a detective. Just might be following in his mother's footsteps." He winked at Nita, who rolled her eyes.

"Let's have a look," she said, and TJ handed her the necklace, which was crusted with dirt. "I don't think we have to worry about fingerprints," she said. "The only

188

ones on there now will be TJ's." She took it to the sink and ran it under the tap. The beads sparkled in her hand.

Grace spread a dishtowel on the table, and Nita laid the necklace on it. Everyone crowded around to look. The clasp was broken, but the string was intact.

"You could be right, TJ," said Nita, "or maybe it was the other lady's, the one in the hospital. Hmm, that gives me an idea." She paused. "If I take this over to the hospital and show it to Ruth, maybe it will jog her memory."

"That's a lot of maybes," said Fitz, "but it's worth a try if Doc Abel says it's okay. You told me he wants her to stay calm, so here's another maybe—maybe he won't like the idea."

"One way to find out," Earl said, and showed Nita to the phone in the front hall.

Abel listened with interest to Nita's proposal, but advised waiting until the next day.

"Actually she looks worse—the bruises are turning yellow—but her overall condition has improved a lot. She's resting nicely now, and I've taken her off the morphine, so she's more coherent. I'll check on her in the morning and let you know if I think she's ready to be questioned again. I'll call the Sea Spray after I finish my morning rounds."

Nita thanked him and rang off. Earl volunteered to drive her to Southampton if Abel gave her the go-ahead. "Just call headquarters and Fred will radio me," he told her.

Eager to pursue her inquiries discreetly, she asked

him, "Did you say anything to Grace about the cause of Metzger's death?"

"No, I didn't mention it, thought it was better not to. Wouldn't want it gettin' all over Bonac before we have more to go on." Grace was one of the more active operators on the gossip hot line, so Earl generally kept his mouth shut when it came to police business, even if it was only petty crime. In a case like this, with a homicide victim and no suspects, it would be extremely unwise to encourage speculation.

"Good," said Nita. "We haven't said anything to TJ, either. So let's keep the dinner conversation to other topics. I'm sure you can entertain us with tales of your exploits in local law enforcement—but please stick to the solved crimes and closed cases."

Earl agreed with a nod and a grin, and they shook hands on it.

THIRTY-SEVEN.

Thursday, August 16

"Toll of Ten Lives in Motor Crashes, One Murder, Saturday," read the front-page headline in the weekly edition of the *East Hampton Star*, the local paper of record. The article led with the story of Pollock and his passengers, including the fact that one of them was dead before the crash.

"Dammit," growled Harry Steele as he slammed the paper down on the breakfast table. In answer to his wife's raised eyebrows, he explained, "Somebody blabbed. Now the cat's out of the bag." He read down the column:

Sunday morning's radio announced that ten people were dead in three Saturday automobile accidents in East Hampton and Southampton, but one victim, a passenger in a car driven by Jackson Pollock, 44, an internationally known artist, was later determined to have been dead when the car ran off Fireplace Road into the woods and overturned.

The victim, Miss Edith Metzger, 25, the assistant manager

of a beauty salon in New York City, was visiting Mr. Pollock, who made his home at The Springs, about a mile from the accident scene. Another passenger in his car, Miss Ruth Kligman, 26, an art gallery assistant in New York City, was taken to Southampton Hospital, where she is recovering from multiple injuries. Mr. Pollock's wife, Lenore Krasner Pollock, also an artist, was in Europe at the time of the accident, which occurred at about 10:15 p.m. on August 11.

Miss Metzger was originally thought to have died of a broken neck at the scene, but was later found to have been fatally strangled not long before the crash. Her death is being investigated as a homicide by the East Hampton Town Police Department, assisted by Captain Brian Fitzgerald and his wife, Detective Juanita Diaz, of the New York City Police Department, who are vacationing here at the Sea Spray Inn.

The article went on to describe the accident scene and paraphrase the police report, although not the Metzger autopsy results. Apparently the reporter didn't get the document itself, but the leak must have come from someone in the coroner's office. And someone at the inn must have given up Fitz's and Nita's names. There was also a description of the funeral tacked onto the end of the article, evidently just before the paper's Wednesday evening deadline. At least they don't have anything on the skin fragments, thought Steele. Small blessing.

He decided to drive over to the Sea Spray with a copy of the paper, and found the Fitzgerald family relaxing on the cottage deck. Another perfect summer day about to be *spoiled,* he said to himself as they waved enthusiastically at his approach.

"Morning, Harry," called Fitz. "To what do we owe the pleasure? Any new developments?"

"I'll say. Take a look at this." He handed over the *Star*.

"Oh, boy, that tears it," said Nita. "I'd better try to get to Kligman before someone at the hospital spills the beans. I know Doc Abel said to wait for his call, but I think we should drive over there now." She looked at Fitz and TJ, who agreed reluctantly to sacrifice their morning on the beach.

"No, you boys stay here, I'll do the honors," offered Steele. "I can pull rank on Doc Abel if necessary. It's time we got to the bottom of this, at least find out what Kligman knows, which I'm sure is plenty."

"I'll just get my handbag," said Nita, "and a piece of evidence you haven't seen yet. Our junior detective here found it yesterday afternoon. I'll explain on the way."

They arrived at the hospital to find Abel conferring with the head nurse at the second-floor charge desk. He saw them coming, and moved to head them off before they could get to Kligman's room.

"Iris is in with her," he explained. "She's sitting up, and she ate a good breakfast. I don't see any reason why you can't talk to her, but I think only Detective Diaz. She might be put off by your uniform, Harry."

Steele chuckled. "Yeah, you're right, Bill. My bedside manner is nonexistent. Besides, Nita here doesn't need any help from me. By the way, who's Iris?"

"Believe it or not, Kligman has an identical twin sister. That's Iris. She looks just like her, at least before the crash. Don't be concerned by the way Ruth looks now—it's just the progression of the bruising. The scrapes on her face are healing nicely. I doubt there'll be any scarring, but she's still somewhat swollen and livid."

Abel asked them to wait while he went to collect Iris.

"Ask her to come see me out here," said Steele. "I'll question her about Ruth's family and friends, get some background, just to keep her occupied for a little while. She may actually have some helpful information she's not aware of. Like who might have had it in for Edith."

Nita greeted Iris with genuine concern as she emerged from the room.

"I'm so glad to learn that your sister's condition has improved," she said. "I hope she'll soon be well enough to go home. I'm sure your mother will be relieved."

"Poor Mamma is in a state," said Iris. "I call her every morning and evening. She needs constant reassurance that Ruthie is on the mend. I haven't told her about Edie—that would be too much for her to take right now. I haven't told Ruthie, either. I just want this nightmare to be over. Besides, I have to get back to work."

"What do you do?" asked Nita.

"I'm a music teacher. I live with Mamma in Newark and

work at home, but I have regular students who come in every week. I took a week off, and I hope it won't be too much longer or they'll find someone else to teach them piano."

With assurance from Abel that he would release Ruth in just a few days, Iris went to join Steele in the hall while the doctor and Nita entered Ruth's room.

Certain that Ruth would have no recollection of their earlier conversation, Nita reintroduced herself and took a seat beside the bed. She could tell that, in spite of her appearance, Ruth was indeed much improved. The IV drip had been removed from her arm, and the back of the adjustable bed had been raised so she could sit in a more comfortable position for meals and conversation.

Before launching into her interrogation, Nita asked Ruth how she was feeling. She wanted to get a sense of how coherent she was, and to put her at ease as much as possible. A little sympathy could go a long way toward encouraging cooperation.

"They're giving me pain pills, but I ache all over. I wish they'd put the drip back in. It made me numb. And they won't let me look in the mirror, but I can feel how cut and bruised my face is. Just look at my arms, all yellow. My whole body's like that—it's horrible!"

Well, thought Nita, *she can talk in complete sentences, and she has a clear idea of her condition.* She decided to reassure her.

"The doctor tells me you're making excellent progress. He says you'll be out of here in no time, but it could take a while for you to get back to normal. You know you had a concussion, right?"

"Yes, he told me. That's why I can't remember what happened."

"When I was here before, you did remember a little. You had a flashback to the moments just before the crash, when the car swerved off the road. Has anything else come back to you? Take your time." Nita held her breath.

Ruth closed her eyes and laid her head back on the pillow. She sighed and ran a hand through her hair. Suddenly her eyes opened wide.

"My hair! Edie! I need her to do my hair; it's a mess. Where is she? She was in the car with us. She came out with me for the weekend. We were going to the concert. Oh, God, everything is so jumbled up." She covered her eyes and winced as her hand touched her injured cheek.

Nita decided that this was the moment. She reached into her handbag, removed the necklace, and held it out so Ruth would see it when she opened her eyes.

"Do you recognize this?" she asked.

Ruth saw it and gasped. "That's Edie's! Nick gave it to her. Where did you get it?"

"From the accident scene," answered Nita, then asked a question of her own. "Who is Nick?"

"Her boss at the Beautique Salon. He's also her boyfriend, but he's married, so Edie's going to break it off." Suddenly she stopped short.

"But she can't. Because she's dead."

THIRTY-EIGHT.

Dr. Abel stepped forward, concerned that Ruth might become agitated, but instead she looked at him calmly, her eyes showing more comprehension than he had seen so far. He nodded encouragement to her and returned to the sidelines.

Nita laid the necklace on the bed, where Ruth could reach it, and prompted her. "Would you like to tell me how you know that?" She held out a hand, and Ruth took it gratefully.

"Yes, it's coming back. I'm still a bit hazy, but seeing Edie's necklace made me remember when I saw her wearing it after she got dressed to go to the concert. I told her how pretty she looked, in her blue dress and the necklace, blue like her eyes. That's what Nick said when he gave it to her—blue to match your eyes. She told me everything about their affair, and of course I understood her problem, since I was seeing a married man, too. We were both in the same boat, except that Jackson said he was going to divorce Lee and marry me. Not like Nick, who wasn't about to leave his wife and kids."

Nita wondered if Edith had been putting pressure on Nick, maybe threatening to rat him out to his wife if he didn't ask for a divorce. Could Nick have decided to solve that problem once and for all?

Ruth reached out to the necklace and ran her fingers over the beads.

"She was all ready to go, but Jackson was taking a nap and I had to get dressed, so I told her she should wait for us downstairs. When I went in to wake Jackson up, he . . . ah . . . didn't want the coffee I brought him." Her look softened, and she glanced at Abel before confiding in Nita, one woman to another. "He wanted to make love." She hesitated, and her gaze turned inward.

"I loved him so much, I couldn't refuse him anything. Certainly not that, even though Edie was waiting. I knew we'd be late for the concert, but I didn't care. It was beautiful, and afterward we lay in each other's arms and swore we'd never let each other go."

She spoke directly to Nita again. "And I won't. He'll be with me forever, for all eternity." Despite her condition, her gift for self-dramatization was intact.

Nita continued to encourage her. "But you decided to go to the concert after all?"

"Yes. We washed up and got dressed and went down to collect Edie. By then it was ten o'clock. We figured that even if we missed the music we could go to the reception after, and she could see Alfonso's fancy mansion and meet some of his famous friends. That's how I sold her on the idea of going. At first she said she wanted to stay home."

"Why? Didn't she like music?"

"Well, the truth is she was afraid to go in the car with Jackson because he'd been drinking. But I convinced her that he'd be okay after he'd had some sleep, so she agreed to go after all."

"So you started out for the concert. Then what happened?"

Ruth frowned and shook her head slowly. The fog was lifting, as if daylight had broken through.

"No, that's not what we did. When we went down, the radio was on but Edie wasn't there. I went into the parlor and turned off the radio, and I knocked on the powder room door in case she was in there, but she wasn't. The back door was open. Jackson said she's probably in the yard, so we . . ."

She broke off. A look of distress crossed her face.

"We didn't see her at first. It was really dark out. She was lying on the ground, over by the studio, clutching at her throat, gasping for breath. Jackson thought she was choking on something. He pushed on her chest a few times, like a lifeguard would do, but nothing came up. He said we'd better get her to the hospital, so he picked her up and carried her to the car. I locked up the house and got in the backseat with her, and Jackson drove off even faster than usual. But he was cold sober, I swear.

"When we got down to the end of Fireplace Road there was a streetlight, and I saw bruises on her neck. She gagged, then she stopped breathing. She died with her head in my lap! Oh, God, I was so scared! I screamed at Jackson to stop the car. He pulled over, and I told him. He looked at her throat, with the pretty blue necklace and ugly red welts around it. We were both just dumbfounded.

"I climbed into the front seat with him and we sat there for a few minutes, trying to figure out what to do. Too late to go to the hospital, and if we did, how would we explain what happened to her? We didn't say it out loud, but we both knew somebody had strangled her. If we took her body to the hospital, they'd think Jackson did it. I couldn't let that happen. I had to think straight.

"I told him we should take her home and put her back in the yard, maybe somewhere more hidden than where we found her. Then call the police and tell them she's missing. That way when they found her, they'd think someone outside assaulted her while we were in the house. We didn't hear anything because the radio was on. And anyway, that's what we thought *did* happen.

"So Jackson turned the car around and headed home. But he was driving way too fast, and he lost control on that curve." With a theatrical gesture, she put her hands to her ears and closed her eyes tight. "I can still hear the tires squealing, and the branches snapping as the car crashed through the woods!"

Ruth sighed deeply, lowered her hands to her lap, and seemed drained of emotion. Apparently her recollection had been a cathartic experience.

"After that," she concluded, "I don't remember anything until I woke up here."

"Of course not," said Nita. "You were thrown out of the car and hit your head. You were in shock and nearly unconscious when we found you on the road. My husband and I saw the accident happen. We stopped, and I gave you first aid at the scene until Dr. Abel arrived and took charge."

"You did? Oh, thank you. But are we finished? I feel a bit faint." Her eyelids fluttered, and Abel stepped up to the bedside and checked her pulse.

"You're doing fine, Ruth," he said, "in fact you're doing extremely well. You're making progress every day. The very fact that your memory has returned is a sign that your brain is healing rapidly." He patted her hand reassuringly. "Now, you get some rest, young lady. Would you like Iris to come back in, or would you rather sleep for a while?"

"I think I'll take a nap now. Please ask Iris to come back later. And tell her I love her," she added as Abel handed her a Percodan tablet with water, cranked down the bed, and adjusted her pillows and blanket.

"Of course. I think she knows how much she means to you, especially now."

Nita stood, and took Ruth's hand again. "You've been extremely helpful, Ruth. I can't thank you enough. We already knew that Edith didn't die in the crash. Now we need to find out who killed her, and why."

THIRTY-NINE.

"Did Iris say anything to you about Edith's boyfriend Nick?" asked Nita as she and Steele headed back to East Hampton.

"No, all we talked about was Ruth. I don't think she knows that much about Edith, just that she and Ruth were roommates and the two of them got on really well. She did say that Ruth was going to a psychiatrist in the city, and that he told her it was okay to be seeing Pollock even though he was married. Iris thought that was bad advice, but of course it was just what Ruth wanted to hear. Her boss at the art gallery had given her the summer off—according to Iris, they close in August anyway—and Ruth couldn't wait to start her 'trial marriage' with Pollock.

"But after a few weeks she was having second thoughts, which is why she went back to town for a couple of days last week. She told Iris she was afraid Jackson was cracking up, and she was having a hard time dealing with his moods."

"I can understand why," said Nita. "According to Jim

Brooks, he was really depressed. How would a twenty-six-year-old girl know what to do about that? Cooped up all alone with him in the house, then snubbed by his friends when he took her out, it's no wonder she needed a break. And why she wanted company. Someone her own age she could talk to when her boyfriend was down in the dumps."

"Or in his cups, more like," observed Steele with a smirk. "From what the neighbors tell me, the man wasn't fit to live with, not lately, anyway. Dan Miller says he'd go through a case of beer every two or three days, and that's not all he was drinking."

"Well, drunk or sober, if we accept Ruth's account, he wasn't responsible for Edith's death," said Nita. She had filled Steele in on their conversation.

"Think she's telling the truth?"

"Yes, I think she is. She could be covering up for Pollock, but in my experience it would be hard for someone to make up such a complicated and detailed story and not give something away, especially after suffering a concussion. Doc Abel is convinced that her amnesia was real, that she wasn't just playing for time so she could come up with a plausible alibi for Pollock. Iris said she didn't tell her Edith was dead, and she seemed genuinely shocked when she realized it on her own. Then it all came back to her.

"Edith's necklace was the key that unlocked her memory, thanks to my son and his canine partner. And to a lucky break. Imagine the trail behind the Finches' house leading right to the accident scene."

"Yep. Walking straight through the woods, you cut off the corner from Gardiner to Fireplace. Good thing Sally's got a sharp nose and TJ's got sharp eyes."

"By the way," Steele continued, "Iris says their father is planning to persuade Ruth to sue Pollock's estate. The auto insurance will pay the hospital bills, but he wants her to go for pain and suffering, lost wages while she's laid up, and psychological injuries."

"What?" Nita was appalled. "I thought Mr. Kligman was out of the picture."

"He is—that's to say he and their mother are separated. From what Iris tells me he's some kind of businessman, sort of a hustler. Swoops in every now and again, takes her or Ruth out to dinner and a show, then drives his fancy car off into the sunset. Only turns up when it suits him. Iris called him to tell him about the accident and right away he sees dollar signs. He knows Pollock was a big-shot artist, so he probably figures he was loaded."

Nita's sympathies were all with Pollock's widow. "Boy, I hope Ruth doesn't go through with it. As if losing your husband isn't bad enough, imagine being dragged into court by the woman he was cheating with when he died."

When they pulled into the parking lot behind the Sea Spray cottages, Nita invited Steele in for a glass of lemonade and a strategy session.

"Let's see if the boys are around. I think we're going to

have to take this investigation into the city, and I'd like to get Fitz's opinion on how best to handle it."

"You think Metzger's boyfriend is a suspect?"

"Sure he is," said Nita. "He would have had a motive if she was putting pressure on him to dump his wife. Suppose she told him to think it over while she was away for the weekend, even gave him the details of where she was going and warned him that she'd spill the beans if he didn't come through when she got back to work on Monday."

She continued to speculate. "So how about the opportunity? He could have followed her out on the train, hung around town until it got dark, even walked up to Springs—plenty of time, and he wouldn't need to take a taxi that could be traced.

"Let's say he gets to the house, finds Metzger alone—she's waiting for Pollock and Kligman to come down, remember—and they go outside to talk things over. But she doesn't see things his way, they start arguing, it turns into a fight, and he decides to shut her up for good. Maybe that was even in the back of his mind all along. What do you think, Harry?"

"I can see that," agreed Steele. "He could have walked back to town and hopped the westbound milk train. Goes through East Hampton at midnight, give or take."

"Milk train?"

"That's the late-night run that collects from the dairies out east and takes the milk into the city for morning delivery. Don't normally take passengers on that run, though every now and again somebody hops on. If he did, the conductor would likely remember him. But even if he did come and go by train, how would he know when she'd be at the house?"

Nita considered the logistics. "Well, he could have gone up to Springs during the day, kept an eye on the place, waiting for his chance to get her alone. Of course if he was just planning to reason with her it wouldn't matter if she was alone, and maybe even a good thing if there were others to back him up, tell her to be sensible and not upset the apple cart."

Steele was skeptical. "How likely is that? There's Kligman, convinced that Pollock is going to get a divorce—why wouldn't she encourage Metzger to hope for the same deal? Even Pollock might side with her, give the guy some man-to-man advice on the benefits of trading in the old model."

"As it happens," Nita reminded him, "again according to Kligman, who I'm inclined to believe, Pollock was taking advantage of those very benefits when Metzger was strangled. And Doc Abel says the medical evidence confirms that Kligman did have sex that night. So the coast was clear for Nick to make his move."

"Who is this Nick, anyway?" asked Fitz, who had just come in from the beach with TJ. Having caught the tail end of Nita's narrative, the boy's ears were burning.

Fitz approached Nita and bent down to give her a kiss

on the forehead, brushing aside a stray curl—a gesture of casual intimacy that brought a smile to Steele's lips. "You two are a great team," he observed.

TJ piped up. "What about me? Dad says I'm a detective, too."

Nita reached over and ruffled his hair affectionately. "And so you are, *Juanito*. Wait 'til you hear how your sleuthing paid off. Let's grab the lemonade and go outside, then Harry and I can put you both in the picture."

Once they were settled on the deck, Nita and Harry recounted the morning's developments. Now that the homicide was front-page news, there was no point in holding back any details from TJ, who soaked it all up avidly. He and Fitz had already been quizzed about it on the beach, and his father was proud of the way TJ handled himself.

"The kid's got the makings, all right," he told Nita. "He's already perfected your skill of talking without saying anything," he teased, earning a poke in the ribs. "What I mean is, he didn't give anything away. You don't have to worry about him blabbing to the other kids. He knows how serious it is, don't you, son?"

Considering the next steps, they agreed it was vital to get the lab report as soon as possible. Chances were it would reveal the killer's blood type, which could be matched against the suspects. So far there were only two— Ted Dragon, with the suspicious scratches on his arm, and Metzger's boss-slash-boyfriend.

"Obviously we need to track down Nick," concluded

Fitz. "This Beautique Salon shouldn't be hard to find. It must be in the phone book. I can take a quick trip into the city and question him, look for any telltale marks."

Nita had a better idea. "How about I call Hector? No offense, honey, but you know what a master interrogator he is, and he's right there in the city." When she worked with Hector Morales on the Lam murder case back in 'forty-three, she had watched him question a prime suspect and marveled at his ability to tell truth from fiction in seemingly noncommittal answers. *El Zorro* was a nickname he had earned many times over.

"Are you kidding?" replied Fitz. "No offense taken. If only you can persuade Hector. Better use the pay phone so we don't alert the whole town." He went inside the cottage and came back with a handful of dimes.

"I'm going back to the station," said Steele, "see if I can get Riverhead to hustle up that report. It's been four days already. They should have it by now."

FORTY.

Lee slept late. She had finally allowed exhaustion to overtake her, leaving the mess from the post-funeral reception to deal with in the morning, but the morning was gone by the time she woke up. Dreading what she would face downstairs, she took her time washing and dressing, but when she finally went down, the place was neat and tidy. Ted, Cile, and Sherry had been there and taken care of everything. There were even fresh flowers in a vase on the breakfast table, and a plate covered with a napkin. She removed the napkin, and found three newly minted Dreesen's donuts.

Somehow this simple thoughtful gesture released the pent-up feelings she had struggled so hard to contain. All through the preparations, the funeral, and the burial she had kept them in check. And last night she had been the perfect hostess, seeing to her guests' every need, dispensing refreshments, accepting commiserations gracefully, comforting others even as she found no comfort in their expressions of sympathy and sorrow. Afterward, those who had been there agreed that her performance was amazing and marveled at her poise and self-control.

Now, alone in the kitchen, staring at a plate of donuts, she felt the floodgates open. She slumped down in a chair, buried her face in her hands, and howled with fury as the tears poured forth. Bile rose into her mouth, carrying with it the grief, anger, pain, regret, and frustration she had been aching to express. She ran to the sink and vomited, heaving up the bitterness she knew would be a lifelong curse.

Let it out, she told herself as her stomach contracted again and again, *get it over with*. Exhausted, she made her way back to the chair and tried to bring her breathing back to normal. Of course it was not over with, there would be many more trials ahead, but at least she wouldn't have an audience. But who was she kidding? From now on she would be under constant scrutiny. The whole art world would be watching to see how she handled the estate. She knew the score—hadn't she been managing Jackson's career ever since the beginning?

Yes, but it was different when he was alive. Even after he began to slide downhill, there was always the chance he'd pull himself together. God knows he tried. The homeopathic remedies, the special diet, the injections, the kosher salt baths, the private clinic, the psychiatrists—something was bound to work.

If only Dr. Heller had lived, she thought ruefully, he would have gotten Jackson back on track. He was the only one who had any success. Just a local G.P., not a specialist, but Edwin Heller kept Jackson off the booze for two years. Jackson trusted him, followed doctor's orders, then Heller had to get himself killed in a goddamned car crash. Even more ironic, he was only forty-four, the same age as Jackson when he died.

This is getting morbid. Pull yourself together and be practical. Jackson may be dead, but by God I'm going to see that his work lives on, that he's right at the top of the heap, up there with Picasso, that old has-been, and Matisse. In fact, he's going to become even more famous, more respected—and his work more valuable.

What was it Sidney said last night? Just leave everything to me. Fat chance! Sure, he knows the market, but he'll have his commission in mind when he's making a deal for top dollar. The price isn't the only consideration—it isn't even the first one. It has to be the right collector, someone with a reputation, not just a fat checkbook. Or the right museum, one that will hang the painting prominently, not just dump it into storage. The cheapskate curators are always crying poor; they just want deep discounts. But if they offer an inducement, like a one-man show, Sidney has to be persuaded to take a smaller cut, maybe even forgo his commission. If something comes up at auction, he has to bid it up even if he winds up buying it himself.

"Meanwhile," she said out loud, "what the hell am I going to live on? I'd better get onto Izzy right away." Apart from the pathetic balance in her bank account, $100 in uncashed traveler's checks, and some loose change in a coffee can in the pantry, she was broke. Her brother Irving would have to ride to the rescue.

She rose and went to the parlor, where the telephone sat on a small mahogany drop-leaf table that friends had given them when they moved in. It was a souvenir of their struggles in the early years, when there was hardly any demand for Pollock's work and they often depended on gifts and loans to get by. Now she needed another loan, a big one, to tide her over until the estate was settled.

The phone was off the hook—another kindness, courtesy of Ted, that had allowed her to sleep undisturbed. Silently thanking him, she depressed the cradle, released it, and got a dial tone. Before dialing her brother's office, she checked her watch and saw that she could make the 2:13 train to the city.

The secretary at the insurance company put her through. Greater New York Mutual was on Madison Avenue at 35th Street.

"I have to see you, Izzy. Now, today. I'm going to take the train to Penn Station and get a cab to your office. I should be there by five thirty, but if I'm late wait for me." She hung up before he could argue.

Her next call was to Schaefer's Taxi. She had over an hour until train time, but she needed to throw a few things in an overnight bag and cash one of the traveler's checks, so she ordered the taxi for one thirty. Len Schaefer would wait for her outside the bank and get her to the station in plenty of time.

She decided she'd better eat something, even though her stomach was far from settled. There was leftover ham and potato salad in the icebox, so she forced some of that down with milk. She wrapped the donuts in tinfoil. *I can share them with Izzy,* she said to herself.

FORTY-ONE.

"*H*ola, Nita, how are you enjoying the beach?"

Inspector Morales was pleased to hear her voice. He missed her, not only because she was a popular member of his team, but also because he could have used her on duty. Domestic disputes in stifling apartments and the occasional gang rumble kept Spanish Harlem's Twenty-third Precinct busy during the hot summer, when school was out and idle youngsters found plenty of ways to get into trouble.

"It's boring, Hector," she replied. "Waves roll in, waves roll out, and then they roll in and out again. All day, all night—talk about monotonous."

Morales laughed. "I guess you'll be glad to get back to your exciting life in the city, where every day is a new adventure."

"Actually," she said, "we're having an adventure right here in East Hampton. There's been a homicide, and Fitz and I are helping the local cops with the investigation."

"*Madre de dios*, girl, don't you two ever take a vacation?"

"Maybe next summer. But seriously, Hector, I wonder if you can do us a real favor." She explained the situation, her story interrupted a couple of times by the operator asking her to deposit more money.

"Hang on a minute, I have the phone book right here," he told her as she slipped another dime into the slot. "Here it is, Beautique Salon, 142 West 57th Street, an easy subway ride downtown. I can be there in half an hour. Give me a number where I can call you later."

"Better call the town police station, ask for Chief Harry Steele. He's in charge of the case." She gave him the number. "Can you believe it? East Hampton Town doesn't have a single detective on the force. I guess they rely on the county cops if there's a case that needs investigating, but I gather this is the first unexplained death they've had in years."

"Kinda refreshing, ain't it?" observed Morales. "Hope it doesn't make you think about moving to the country."

"What would I do with myself? Like I said, no detectives out here. I'd have to open a *restaurante* and try to sell the locals on Cuban food." That prompted a chuckle at the other end of the line.

The operator asked for another dime, so Nita thanked Morales, wished him good hunting, and rang off.

When she got back to the cottage, Steele had left for the station, and Fitz and TJ had changed out of their bathing suits.

"I think we've done everything we can for now. Harry will work on getting the lab report, and Hector will question this Nick character. I told him to look for scratch marks. So what do you say we take the afternoon off? Hector was teasing me about working on vacation, and of course he's right. We're supposed to be off duty."

"Listen here, Detective Diaz," scolded her husband, "you're always the one who gets to solve interesting crimes, while I'm stuck behind a desk half the time and spend the other half breaking up bar fights and booking drug dealers. You wouldn't begrudge me a little detecting experience, would you?"

"Me too!" added TJ, and Nita shook her head in sympathy.

"All right, Junior G-Man, and you, too, Dick Tracy, we'll all detect together. Harry says we make a great team and you know, I think he's right." She gave them both a hug.

"But right now we can take a break while we wait for more evidence. Sometimes a detective's most important asset is patience. Remember Ted said TJ should come back to The Creeks so he can taste the bread he helped make? I wonder if the coast is clear over there now. Let's find out."

Her suggestion was received with enthusiasm, and they headed to the inn to use the phone.

Emerging from the BMT station at 57th Street and Seventh Avenue, Hector Morales had only a half-block walk to reach the Beautique Salon. Before entering, he checked the interior through the window and saw that it was quiet. Not much business early on a Thursday afternoon—one woman having her hair permed by the single beautician on duty, and another in curlers under the dryer. A bored receptionist was reading *Photoplay*.

The sight of a large unfamiliar man in front of her desk got her attention. "Hiya, mister. Lookin' for somebody?" She was sure he wasn't there for a haircut or a manicure.

"Yes, miss, I'd like to see the manager, if he's available." Even kept discreetly low, his rich baritone voice resonated with authority. She figured him for a salesman.

"Name, please," she said as she lifted the intercom speaker. He told her, without mentioning that he was a police inspector, and he heard a received buzz in a room at the back of the salon.

"There's a man out here to see ya, Mr. Petrillo," she said, and Morales heard him reply, "What does he want?" She looked up and raised her eyebrows.

"It's about Miss Metzger," he told her.

"Oh, gee, it's terrible what happened," said the receptionist. "Poor Edie. A car crash, of all things. Her what only rode the subway." She relayed the information to her boss, who said to send the man in.

"The door at the rear, Mr. Morales. Says 'office' right on it." He thanked her and walked to the back.

Petrillo, eh? he thought as he approached the door. *Italian, Catholic, therefore no divorce. Metzger was holding out false hope.*

He knocked and was told to come in. The room was small and cluttered, made even more cramped by a large couch, which Morales assumed had been the scene of numerous Petrillo-Metzger assignations.

The manager, a man of medium height in his midthirties, his black hair lightly salted with gray at the temples, stood up from his desk chair and offered Morales his hand. His grip was firm but not aggressive. *Plenty of power there if he chose to use it,* mused the inspector. He directed Morales to a chair opposite the desk. From that position he could see the back of a framed photograph, presumably of Mrs. Petrillo, maybe with a child or two. He could imagine Petrillo slipping it into a drawer before inviting Metzger into the office.

Petrillo offered him a cigarette, which he declined, then took one for himself. He had removed his jacket and tie and had his sleeves rolled up, so it was easy for Morales to see that there were no wounds on his face, neck, or forearms.

"Are you here about the insurance?" he asked. "I told Miss Metzger's mother I thought it would cover the funeral. I hope I was right about that."

"No, sir, I'm afraid it's nothing to do with insurance." He took out his shield, displayed it, and identified himself.

Petrillo froze. He stared at the shield, then at Morales. He stubbed out the cigarette.

"What do you want?" His tone was guarded.

Not wanting to jump to conclusions, Morales could

tell that Petrillo was worried. *Could be only that he doesn't want his wife to find out about the affair, or could be he has something more to hide.* He considered how to phrase his questions so as to get the most information while revealing the least.

"As you know," he said, "Edith was killed in East Hampton. The local police have asked me to follow up on a few points that need clarifying."

"Such as?"

"Did you know where she was going for the weekend?"

"Yeah. She told me she and her roommate were going to visit the roommate's boyfriend in the country. Out on the Island, East Hampton, she said."

"Do you know the roommate?"

"Ruth? Sure. She comes in here to get her hair done. That's how she and Edie—Miss Metzger, I mean—how they met."

"We can call her Edith, or Edie if you prefer. When I asked if you knew where she was going, I meant specifically."

"You mean the address? No, but she did say it's in a little backwater outside of town, as if East Hampton itself isn't a backwater. I've been there a couple of times, driving through on the way to go fishing in Montauk. Wide spot in the highway, that's all it is."

Petrillo had relaxed a bit. *So he has a car,* thought Morales. He had noticed the salon's hours posted on the entrance door, informing patrons that the shop closed at six p.m. on Saturdays. If Petrillo's car was handy—and there was plenty of on-street parking at the weekends—he could have locked up, hopped in the car, scooted over the Queensboro Bridge at 59th Street, and been in East Hampton by nine o'clock. He'd have to have known where to find Edith, even if he says he didn't.

Morales kept his tone mild and even, very matter-of-fact. "Did she say how long she'd be gone?"

"She said she was planning to come back Sunday night, but if she decided to stay another day she'd call and let me know. We're closed on Mondays, so she couldn't have stayed over if she'd wanted to." He blinked hard and ran his hand over his face. "Oh, man. I'm sorry. It was just such a shock. Edie was a real sweet kid."

"I understand, Mr. Petrillo. I don't mean to distress you, but as I said, there are some loose ends we need to tie up."

"Yes, of course, whatever I can do. But I don't get what you're driving at."

"Did you take the weekend off, too?"

"Not likely. Especially since Edie was off. Even in the summer, Saturday is our busiest day, and I can't afford to turn away business. If we have a lot of walk-ins I have to take over the reception desk so the girl can tend to customers."

"So you were here all day last Saturday?"

"Isn't that what I just said? What is this?"

"What time did you leave?"

Now Petrillo was getting anxious. "I locked up a little after six, like usual. So what?"

"Did you drive to work on Saturday?"

"I never drive to work. I live in Astoria, so I take the Number 8 right to the corner here. But what's that got to do with Edie?"

Could be he's genuinely confused by these questions, said Morales to himself, *or he's hiding something. Okay, no scratch marks, but they haven't yet determined whose skin was under Metzger's nails. Could be she scratched herself in the struggle. So for now Petrillo is definitely a suspect.*

Morales decided to level with him.

"I'll be frank with you, Mr. Petrillo. Edith Metzger was not killed in the automobile accident. She was already dead when the car crashed. We know you were having an affair with her. Do you see why I need to find out where you were when she died?"

Petrillo stared at him in horror.

"Holy shit!" He repeated himself, softer this time. "Holy shit."

FORTY-TWO.

"What's the matter with your face?" asked Lee as she settled herself in a chair opposite her brother's desk. She'd spent the three-hour train ride from East Hampton refining a list of questions she had for him, but that wasn't one of them.

Reflexively, Irving reached his hand up to the bandage under his left eye. "It's nothing, just a shaving cut," he told her. "Almost healed now."

Lee looked at him skeptically. "Since when do you shave your cheekbone? And don't tell me you ran into a door." Still miffed that he hadn't attended the funeral, and with another grievance simmering as well, she hadn't embraced him when she entered the office.

Irving dissembled. "Really, it's just a scratch. It's kind of embarrassing—I'm not sure how I did it, maybe in my sleep. I've been restless lately, worried about you."

His effort to divert her was successful, although she

did make him promise to change the dressing when he got home. He waved off her concern and asked her what she needed from him right now. She decided to leave the loan request until after they had discussed some practical matters.

"The insurance. I want to be sure everything is fully covered. What happens if the studio goes up in flames? I'm afraid that fucking kerosene stove is going to blow up. I told Jackson not to put it in, but he insisted. He thought he was going to work out there in the winter, but he never did. He'd fire it up when it got chilly and I was sure he'd burn the place down."

"You're right to be concerned. As it stands now, the policy probably would not pay out the full market value if everything were destroyed. I'd say you have two options. Either get the stove taken out and keep the building locked, or move all the art into storage. That's more expensive, but the premium will go down, so it may balance out."

"Do I need to have everything appraised? It's a few years since the policy was written, and the prices have risen quite a bit."

"I strongly recommend it, Lee, especially if you leave the paintings in the studio. In any case, you need an inventory so we can update the coverage. There must be more work since we wrote the policy." He flipped open a file on his desk. "It's dated November 1, 1952, nearly four years ago."

Lee shook her head. "Oh, Izzy, what can I tell you? There was hardly any more work after that. It broke my heart to see him so inactive. I don't think there can be more than a dozen paintings that aren't on the 1952 inventory. Most of what he did these past couple of years was reworking earlier things."

"Well, that will have to be accounted for. The policy won't pay out twice for the same canvas. Plus I'm sure some of the things on the old inventory have been sold, so they need to come off."

"That's right," she said. "Fred Olsen bought *Blue Poles*—one of the biggest paintings Jackson ever did—for six thousand dollars. He was thrilled, especially when he deposited his four-thousand-dollar share in the bank—Janis takes a third. And Ben Heller is buying *One*, another big canvas, for eight thousand, though he hasn't finished paying it off yet."

"You have to check with Janis to find out what he has at the gallery or in storage. That won't be covered by your policy."

It was time for Lee to bring up the matter of her immediate financial needs. *Better come right out with it*, she decided. *No point beating around the bush.*

"Listen, Izzy, I need a favor. Like I said, Ben owes me money for the painting, but I don't know when he'll pay up, and I have bills to pay right now. I was shocked when I found out there's only about $350 in the bank. I owe Alfonso for the funeral, the appraisal will cost something, and I'll have other expenses while the estate is settled. I need a loan."

"How much?"

"Five thousand should tide me over."

Irving had been expecting something like this, though not quite such a large sum. He sat back in his chair and let the moments tick by as he figured out how much he could afford.

"I want to help you," he told her, "but I can't do that much all at once. I can let you have a thousand now, and more later if you need it. I'll have to cash in some bonds. I'll go to the bank tomorrow morning and have them transfer the funds to your account in East Hampton. You should have the thousand by Monday."

Lee let out a sigh. She was disappointed not to get all she asked for, but she could hardly seem ungrateful. Even a thousand was a big help. Alfonso wouldn't press her, and Gerry Weinstock's attorney's fee wasn't due right away.

"Thank you, Izzy. I'll pay you back, with interest. You know there'll be plenty once I have clear title to Jackson's work."

"I only wish it could be more. Maybe after the first of the month I can do better. Let's see how it goes."

He changed the subject. "By the way, do you have someone looking after the place while you're in town?"

"Yes, Cile and Sherry. I think you've met them; they live just up the road. They're taking care of Gyp and

Ahab, and I asked them to make sure everything is secure overnight. I'll go back tomorrow. Gerry is coming out for the weekend, and I have to meet with him about the will."

Irving approved. "Good. Gerry will know how to protect your assets." He glanced at her overnight bag. "Now let's get some dinner and I'll take you back to my place."

"Thanks all the same, but I can't face the subway ride to Brooklyn. I made a reservation at the Earle for tonight. Let's grab a cab downtown and we can eat there."

Secretly glad that she had let him off the hook, he went around the desk and took her hand as she rose from the chair.

"This is such an ordeal. You must be all in. My poor little Lena," he said, reverting to her birth name, which she had long ago renounced in favor of the more poetic Lenore.

Hoping to comfort her, he wrapped her in his arms, and she slumped against him. At five foot four, she came up to his shoulder, where she rested her head. She made no sound, but he could feel her sobbing silently. When she eased back and looked up at him, he saw the tears in her eyes—tears of sorrow, but also of anger and regret.

"If only you had gotten to her, Izzy! Why didn't you get her out of there, away from him? That slut actually moved into *my* house. She was eating off *my* dishes, shitting in *my* toilet, sleeping in *my* bed—with *my husband*, for Christ's sake! I told you to put a stop to it. Why didn't you?"

Of course she was mad at him, who wouldn't be?

When she called him long-distance from Paris a week ago, he had promised to go to Springs and remove Ruth Kligman from the house.

"How do you know she's there?" he had asked.

"I got a cable from May."

Lee's friendship with May Rosenberg went back a long way—back to the 1930s, when she was living with Igor. For a time they had shared an apartment with May and her husband Harold, a writer who had since become an influential art critic. It was partly because the Rosenbergs had a summer place in Springs that Lee and Jackson bought a house nearby, and they remained close in spite of Harold's ambivalence about Jackson's radical abstract paintings. A few years ago, in an infuriating article he had described them as "apocalyptic wallpaper," a real slap in the face. Okay, he hadn't actually named Jackson as the perpetrator, but everyone knew whom he had meant.

Lee had distanced herself from Harold after that, and openly mocked his criticism as hackwork, but she was still sympathetic to May, an aspiring writer who was as much in her husband's shadow as Lee was. And like Jackson, Harold was unfaithful, so there was an additional common bond between the two beleaguered wives. It was no wonder, then, that May would alert Lee to the fact that her home had been turned into a love nest for Jackson's infidelity.

The cablegram had been waiting for her when she returned to her Paris hotel after visiting friends in the

South of France. When she read it—RUTH KLIGMAN LIVING WITH JACKSON STOP. SHE IS IN YOUR PLACE STOP—she had felt the blood rush to her head and her guts go into spasm. But it quickly occurred to her that, instead of acting as a well-meaning friend, May was taunting her, paying her back for the spiteful things she'd said about Harold. Then she was overwhelmed with bitterness. What could she possibly do about it from three thousand miles away?

It wasn't long before her frustration turned to resolve. Even if she was powerless to intervene personally, she wasn't without recourse. None of her friends could be trusted—she didn't know which of them would take Jackson's side and which would be loyal to her—but she could trust her brother.

She reserved a transatlantic call for two a.m. to his home number. It would be eight p.m. in Brooklyn. A bachelor, he could be found at home most evenings, buried in a book or listening to his large collection of jazz records.

Irving would do what she would have done if she'd been there. Evict the bitch.

But he hadn't done it. Why not?

"I couldn't just drop everything and rush out there," he explained now. "I had to wait until the weekend, and I couldn't get a car on Saturday. The rental agency didn't have anything until Sunday, and by then it was too late. I was all ready to go on Sunday morning when I got the call from Alfonso about the accident."

He gave her another hug. "How was I to know—no one could have known—that Jackson would choose last Saturday night to self-destruct? It could have happened any time, you must realize that."

Lee was not mollified. "I'm sorry, Izzy, I can't get over it just like that. What I realize is that Jackson is dead, and so is that other slut who was along for the ride." She hadn't picked up the *Star* that morning, so she didn't know Metzger was already dead when they crashed. "Meanwhile slut number one is still alive. I hope every bone in her body is broken!"

Irving decided to change the subject again.

"It's getting late. Let's get you down to the Earle and checked in, then we can find a nice restaurant in the Village. Remember when we used to hang out with the bohemian crowd at Romany Marie's on Eighth Street? I wonder if it's still there."

With working-class parents who had no interest in the arts, Irving had been the exception among the older Krasner children. As the family intellectual, he was a beacon to the renegade young Lena. He introduced her to philosophy, poetry, and jazz; encouraged her to be an artist; and took her to the Greenwich Village haunts that would become her inspiration, her refuge, and her spiritual home.

Chief among them was Romany Marie's, where the intelligentsia had been drinking, arguing, plotting revolutions, and instigating love affairs since before the First

World War. The owner, Marie Marchand, a genuine Romanian gypsy, lived up to her peripatetic heritage.

"She kept moving," reminisced Lee. "Christopher Street, Minetta Street, Grove Street, Washington Place, West Fourth Street, West Eighth Street—she was literally all over the downtown map. Last I heard she was running the café in the Hotel Brevoort, just off Washington Square. That's only a couple of blocks from the Earle. Let's go find out if she's still in business."

Irving picked up her overnight bag before she had a chance to grab it.

"Let me get that," he said. "It's the least I can do."

FORTY-THREE.

Back in his office at the Twenty-third Precinct, Hector Morales put through a call to the East Hampton Town Police.

"I don't think Nick Petrillo is your man, Harry," he told Chief Steele after introducing himself. "It may have been humanly possible, but only if he had his car handy." He outlined the scenario in which Petrillo drove to Springs in time to confront Metzger, fight with her, and strangle her before Pollock and Kligman found her in the yard at around ten p.m.

"He says he didn't drive to work on Saturday, and the girls at the salon back him up. They say he was there all day, locked up just after six, they all left together, and he walked with one of them to the subway station at 57th and Seventh. She went to the downtown platform, and he went to the uptown platform headed to Queens. His train came in before hers, and she saw him get on.

"But suppose, instead of riding home to Astoria, he gets off at Queensboro Plaza, where he's parked the car. From there it's a straight run down Northern Boulevard and out to the Island. Three hours, easy."

"But you don't think that's what happened."

"No, I don't. He said his wife had the car, took the kids to the beach that day. That's easy enough to check. Besides, he shows no signs of having struggled with Metzger, no visible scratches or bruises. I wouldn't rule him out entirely at this stage, but my instinct tells me you're looking for someone else."

"He could have rented a car," suggested Steele.

"Yes, I thought of that, in which case there'll be a record of it. I can have inquiries made if you like."

"Let's hold off on that for now. First I want to get the tissue analysis results, find out the blood type from the skin samples. I'm hoping to rule out Metzger herself, then decide where to go next. Pollock had an unusual blood type, so a match would make him a high probability. If that happens we need to question Kligman more intensively. And we need to draw blood from other suspects, including Petrillo, in case one of them turns out to be a match."

"Call me when you want me to move on him," said Morales. Steele thanked him for his cooperation and said he'd be in touch. He hung up, flipped the intercom switch, and buzzed Fred Tucker.

"Call Riverhead again. Find out what's holding up

that damned report. They said it'd be ready this after-noon, and it's almost five now."

Just then the phone on Fred's desk rang. He excused himself and answered it, to find a technician from the Suffolk County Medical Laboratory on the line.

"I was about to call you," he said. "Do you have the Metzger results? Great. Let me put you through to Chief Steele." He returned to the intercom and told his boss to pick up.

"Chief Steele? This is Conroy, from the Suffolk Lab. I have the report you were asking for."

"About time," grumbled Steele. "Were you able to identify a blood type?"

"Yes. The tissue had enough blood in it to get a result. It's A positive, quite common, second only to O positive. I'll put the full report in the mail to you. I already gave a copy to Dr. Nugent." Naturally the coroner's office would be keeping tabs on the investigation.

Steele thanked the technician and hung up the phone. The test ruled out Pollock, with his rare Type A nega-tive blood. He opened the file and checked the Metzger autopsy report. Like Kligman, she was Type O positive, so it wasn't her own skin or Kligman's under her nails. She had wounded her attacker, all right, badly enough to draw blood.

He was going to have to get samples from Nick Petrillo and Ted Dragon, and maybe Ossorio, too, while he was at it. Petrillo was the obvious candidate—maybe she scratched him on the shoulder or upper arm, where a long-sleeve shirt would cover it. Notwithstanding Dragon's wounded forearm, he and Ossorio were less likely, so he was hoping to eliminate them. He buzzed Fred and asked him to get Dr. Abel on the phone.

"I can help you with Ossorio," Abel told him. "He came to me a year or so ago complaining of fatigue, so I ran a blood test. Turns out he was slightly anemic. I prescribed an iron tonic and he improved. Hold the phone a minute while I check the file."

It didn't take Abel long to come back on the line. "He's O positive, the most common type among Spanish and Chinese, and he's part both."

"How about Dragon?"

"He's not a patient of mine. Maybe he goes to Dr. Cooper, or maybe he hasn't had the need since he's been living out here. Do you want me to test him?"

"First let me try Cooper. If he has nothing on file I'll call you back."

Dr. Cooper was with a patient, but his nurse said she'd check to see if Edward Dragon was on the roster. He was not. Apparently he hadn't thought the scratches on his arm were serious enough to seek medical treatment. Even if he had, there would be no reason for a doctor to draw blood.

Steele called Abel back and asked him to meet him at The Creeks. Better do it now and get it over with.

When the chief arrived he found Fitz's car parked in

the driveway. The Pollock family—Stella, Sande, Arloie, and the kids—had left earlier that afternoon, so the Fitzgeralds had taken up Ted's offer of a return visit.

The front door was wide open, as was the dining room door to the terrace, where the hosts and their guests were feasting on thick slices of Ted's home-baked bread, liberally buttered and heaped with local beach plum jelly, washed down with iced tea.

What trusting fellows, thought Steele as he walked past valuable art and artifacts. *Anyone could just drive up and help himself. Still, I suppose they can afford to part with a few of these knickknacks, and no one would want the ugly abstract paintings. Nothing but smears and blotches.*

On the wall beside the dining room door, he was confronted by one of Ossorio's recent creations, with several glass eyes and a deer's jawbone embedded in its thickly impastoed surface. *You couldn't pay me to steal that*, he said to himself as he eased warily past it and out onto the terrace.

"Hail to the chief!" cried Ted as Steele approached the party. "Pull up a chair, dig in, and give us a report. Any news that wasn't in the paper?" He and Alfonso rose politely, and remained standing as Steele did. He also refused refreshments.

"I suppose Nita has told you that her colleague in the city is doing some legwork for us," he began, and Nita nodded in agreement. "Well, he questioned Metzger's boss, Nick, and the man is definitely a suspect."

TJ was the first to react. "¡Ay, *caramba!* Really? Isn't he the guy who gave her the necklace I found?"

"Yessir, that's him. He has an alibi of sorts, but it doesn't put him in the clear. Inspector Morales has some more checking to do. Meanwhile our Mr. Petrillo—that's Nick's last name—is number one on the list."

Nita picked up on Steele's implication: there was still an active list. She had been hoping Hector would nail it down, but evidently his investigation so far wasn't conclusive. She wanted to hear the details, but not in front of Alfonso and Ted.

"Any other leads?" asked Ted, eager for more inside information.

This was just a bit awkward. Steele mumbled something vague about promising lab results. He was trying to figure out how to ask Ted for a blood sample without putting him on the defensive when Dr. Abel arrived with his medical bag in hand.

Well, thought Steele, *I guess I'll have to come clean.* He told them that the blood type had been identified, and that anyone who had come in contact with Metzger would have to be tested.

Alfonso and Ted watched as Dr. Abel opened his bag, removed a small kit, and placed it on the table. They looked at each other, and at Steele.

Alfonso spoke. Gone was the conviviality of the social gathering, replaced by an air of offended dignity.

"I believe we both told Detective Diaz that we did not

see Jackson, Ruth, or Edith Metzger on the evening of the accident," he said in a frosty tone. "There would be no reason, no reason at all, for us to be tested."

"With all due respect, Mr. Ossorio, I have only your word for that."

The response from Alfonso was a withering glare. "I see," he said. It was as if an iceberg had just beached on the shore of Georgica Pond and cast a frigid pall over the terrace.

Without another word, he sat down at the table and held out his left hand.

The doctor opened his kit and took out a small glass pipette, a sterile needle, and an alcohol swab. He wiped the tip of Alfonso's middle finger, pricked it, and squeezed out a drop of blood, which he collected in the pipette. He sealed the sample in a test tube already labeled AO. He pressed the swab onto Alfonso's fingertip and folded his hand into a fist. Of course this was redundant, since he already knew Alfonso's blood type, but by sampling both men it would not look as if Ted were being singled out.

The Fitzgerald family made themselves as inconspicuous as possible.

Abel kept his eyes on his work, avoiding Alfonso's glacial stare. When he stood up and stepped away from the table, Ted took his place and the procedure was repeated. His sample went into a test tube marked ED.

"I appreciate your cooperation, gentlemen," said Steele,

hoping to ease the tension. "This is purely routine, and no reflection on your veracity, you understand."

"I understand perfectly, Chief Steele," said Alfonso. "I think you and Dr. Abel have everything you need, so you may now leave our home."

"I think it's time for us to head out as well," said Fitz after a cool breeze had blown Steele and Abel away. He was sure the mood would not be turning around just because they had left.

Ted tried to dissuade them. "Honestly, please don't feel you need to hurry off. Alfonso has thin skin, as you see. The chief was only doing his job."

"I'm so glad you understand," said Nita, turning to Ossorio. "He has his hands full with this case, and very little experience with homicide investigations. He just wants to be certain he doesn't neglect or overlook anything. Try to see it from his point of view. Jackson and the girls were headed here. He can't just accept your assurance that they never arrived."

She flashed her trademark smile, guaranteed to melt the hearts of the opposite sex, hoping it would work as effectively on a homosexual as it did on straight men. "Besides, in my professional opinion, *ves culpable como el pecado*. Guilty as sin."

Alfonso thawed. "Nita, *mi querida*, God knows I am indeed a sinner. But I am not a killer. At least not yet. If Steele comes back, I just may strangle him."

She slipped her arm through Alfonso's as they walked to the door. "When this is all over, send a nice fat check to the police benevolent fund," she whispered. "Then all your sins will be forgiven."

FORTY-FOUR.

Friday, August 17

"Have you seen the *Star*?" asked Len Schaefer as he opened the taxi door for Lee. He was waiting to pick her up at the station, as per her order of the previous day. She had taken the morning train back to East Hampton, arriving at 11:28, resigned to dealing with the studio inventory as soon as possible.

"When did I have time to get the paper yesterday?" she answered brusquely, a tone unwarranted by Schaefer's remark.

"No, I s'pose not," he said. "Here, take mine." He handed her the paper from the front seat as she took her place in back.

No sooner had the cab crossed the tracks and headed toward Springs than Schaefer heard his passenger muttering and swearing. By the time they pulled into her driveway, Lee was boiling.

"For Christ's sake, Len, you could have warned me! It's

bad enough the little bitch was killed, but before the accident? Now they'll be accusing Jackson of murder, not just drunk driving. What a fucking nightmare—as if I don't have enough to deal with!"

Schaefer tried to calm her down. "Take it easy, Mrs. Pollock. Nobody's sayin' your husband killed her."

"Want to bet?" she retorted angrily. "What do you think everybody is going to assume after they read this? Which everybody has by now."

She could feel her intestines beginning to react. She threw the paper back into the taxi, slammed the door, opened her purse and shoved the fare into Schaefer's hand, grabbed her overnight bag, and fled to the house.

Raging internally, she let herself in, dropped her bag, and stormed to the telephone. Her anger was complicated by a sense of dread as doubt entered her mind. *Could Jackson actually have done it? Thank God this didn't come out until after the funeral,* she thought. *I have to find out what's going on.*

She dialed the town police station. Fred put her through to Chief Steele, who had been expecting her call. Not knowing that she had gone to the city without reading the paper, he was surprised it had taken her so long to react to the *Star* story.

She demanded a full review of the investigation—understandable under the circumstances, though he was wishing she wasn't demanding it quite so loudly—and insisted he come to her. She had no car, the taxi was gone, and she had no intention of calling it back. Nor did she want to be seen in town, where she would be the object of public curiosity, pity, and other less charitable sentiments.

Steele understood her situation and agreed to a private interview as soon as he could get away. "How soon?" she demanded, and he promised to be with her in less than an hour.

Dr. Abel had called earlier to let him know that Ted Dragon's blood was Type O negative, commonly known as the universal donor. He had also mentioned, as they left The Creeks, that Ted's scratches really did look like they were made by rose thorns, not fingernails. So Steele crossed him off the list and had a call put through to Hector Morales. He found the inspector at his desk in the Twenty-third Precinct.

"I think we should follow up with Petrillo," said Steele. "We need a blood sample, and a photograph."

"I'll see if I can get him to come up here. We can type his blood right here in the station. I'll tell him. That way his staff at the salon won't have to know what's going on. I think he'll cooperate, otherwise I'll go down there with the police surgeon and photographer, which would be just a little bit embarrassing for him."

"Let me know as soon as you can. Meanwhile I have one very irate widow to deal with. She flipped her lid when she read the newspaper article. At least I can tell Mrs. Pollock that her late husband is in the clear, though she won't like hearing the details of his alibi."

"Maybe you can skip the part where he was screwing his girlfriend when her roommate was being strangled," advised Morales. "The fact that his blood doesn't match what was under Metzger's nails should be enough to set her mind at rest."

"Yeah, I guess so, though I wouldn't put it quite like that. I don't think her mind will be at rest for a long time, if ever. She's wound pretty tight."

Before heading up to Springs, Steele made a detour to the Sea Spray. There was no one at the cottage, so he left a note to let Nita and Fitz know that Petrillo was now the number one suspect. He really didn't need to be in touch with them at this stage, since he had no results to report— he was procrastinating.

It was another perfect beach day, with a cloudless blue sky and a balmy breeze that mitigated the heat shimmering off the sand. The Fitzgeralds certainly had luck with the weather for their vacation, even if they hadn't been able to take full advantage of it. Suppressing the urge to borrow a bathing suit from the inn's supply, strip off his uniform, and go for a dip in the cool ocean, Steele reluctantly walked back across the baking tarmac to the patrol car and turned north.

Lee was waiting for him on the back porch, sitting on her cast-iron bench with an empty coffee cup and a full ashtray. She marched down to meet him as soon as his car came to a stop, and opened the conversation on a hostile note.

"You took your time," she growled, "what the hell kept you?"

Keep it cordial, Harry, he said to himself. *Don't take it personally, she's in a state—who wouldn't be?*

"I'm sorry, Mrs. Pollock," he began, "I had an urgent matter to attend to. I'm hoping it will lead to a break in the case. I'll explain everything, but first I want to offer my condolences. I know what a shock this has been for you. Please accept my sincere sympathy."

It was a standard commiseration, but Steele delivered it with conviction and Lee accepted it with tempered thanks.

"I appreciate your kind thoughts, but what I'd appreciate even more is a full account of what happened, and what you're doing to clear my husband's name. Please come in." She led him to the back door, ushered him in, and offered him a seat at the kitchen table.

Lee lit a cigarette, leaned back stiffly in her chair, and gazed steadily at the chief.

"Let's have it," she demanded.

He had been framing his report as he drove to the house, wanting to give her as much information as possible without compromising the investigation. First, however, he needed to reassure her.

"From the information we've gathered so far, it looks like your husband was not responsible for Edith Metzger's death." That wasn't an all-out exoneration, since there was always a chance he was involved in some way, either as a witness or an accomplice, but it was true, and it had the desired effect.

Lee let out a huge sigh and visibly relaxed. "Thank God," she murmured. She slumped in the chair, as if an iron rod had been removed from her spine.

"In all other respects," Steele continued, "the *Star* gives just as full a report of the accident as I can. But without intending to, the article made it appear as if Mr. Pollock might have killed her before the accident. To be honest, that did seem to be a possibility. But we now have evidence that points in a different direction."

"What evidence? What direction?"

"I can't go into detail because the investigation is active. Let me just say that we hope to have some answers very soon."

Lee was far from satisfied by such generalities. "What's that supposed to mean? If Jackson didn't do it, you must have some idea who did by now. It's been almost a week." She was getting testy again.

"Please understand my position, Mrs. Pollock. If I seem evasive"—and here she snorted and interjected, "I'll say"—"it's only because I have nothing definitive to report. As soon as I do, believe me, I'll fill you in. Right now I can't say anything that might compromise the case. It's complicated enough as it is."

She sat and smoked in silence for a few moments, considering his situation for the first time. If she appeared to be meddling, it might cast doubt on Jackson's innocence, though that word was only appropriate in the narrowest sense. He was guilty of many reprehensible things, but apparently not of murder. For the moment, she decided, it was best to leave it at that.

"Listen, Harry," she said, her tone softer and more reasonable, "I know you're in a spot. I'm sorry to be so pushy. I'm not forgetting the times you or one of your men saw to it that Jackson got home in one piece. Please bear with me. This past week has been one long bad dream. I want to put it all behind me, you know?"

"Of course you do. So do I. One thing I can tell you is that Fitzgerald and Diaz, the two New York City police officers, have been a godsend. They're really helping to move the investigation along. As you know, Mr. Pollock's passengers were out from the city for the weekend, so we're following up on that end with their assistance."

"Yes, I read in the paper that they were on the case. It's funny, their names rang a bell. I'm sure I've run into them before, must've been in the city, but I can't remember where or when. Maybe it'll come back when I'm thinking a bit straighter. Right now I've got other things on my mind."

She got up, opened the back door for Steele, and thanked him as he left.

"It was good of you to come. You've taken a great weight off my shoulders. You won't mind, will you—I mean it won't cause you any problems—if I tell anyone who insinuates that Jackson killed that girl that you say he didn't?"

"Well," he hedged, "I didn't exactly say that, but you can tell them we have evidence to the contrary."

"Goddammit, Harry, you sound like a lawyer. Speaking of which, I need to call Gerry Weinstock and remind him to bring the will out with him tomorrow. I'm going to be in charge of Jackson's estate, and managing it will be a big job."

"You can handle it, Mrs. Pollock," he assured her with complete confidence.

After a stop at home for lunch, Steele returned to the station to find a note on his desk. All it said was "Petrillo O+." Cross off suspect number one, and that takes care of the whole list—Pollock, Kligman, Ossorio, Dragon, and now Petrillo. The investigation had just hit a wall.

FORTY-FIVE.

The Fitzgerald family had decided to visit Guild Hall's annual invitational exhibition by artists of the region—which was, as usual, a reflection of the cultural center's split personality.

At one extreme were the conservatives, an odd-bedfellows mixture of wealthy summer folks and old-family locals who resisted change in all things cultural as well as social, political, and gastronomic. When they attended any of Guild Hall's many arts events, they wanted music you could hum along to, poetry that rhymed, movies and plays with plenty of laughs and happy endings, and pictures of familiar scenery, attractive people, pretty floral arrangements, and thoroughbred animals.

At the other end of the spectrum were the radicals who believed that the old barn needed a thorough airing out. They wanted fare that challenged rather than satisfied—progressive jazz, Beat poetry, Brecht and Beckett instead of drawing room comedy, experimental cinema, preferably European or Japanese, and abstract art, the more incomprehensible the better. Ever since 1949, when the spatter-and-daub school first invaded, the landscapists and flower painters had been on the defensive and were not beating a quiet retreat.

Trying to please as wide an audience as possible, Guild Hall's beleaguered administration was engaged in a perpetual balancing act, nowhere better illustrated than in the annual invitational. Dubbed the Art Wars by the *Star*'s art critic, the show always provoked heated debate between the Old Guard and vanguard factions and their fans. "So far at least," wrote the critic, "all the bloodshed has been verbal. There will be violence, but it will exhaust itself in a few well-worn phrases, such as every museum guard knows by heart."

Unaware of the long-running controversy, Nita, Fitz, and TJ visited Guild Hall with open minds and eyes recently opened by Ossorio. As they entered the lobby, which also served as the theater's foyer, they had a choice of turning right or left into one of the two flanking galleries. The double doors on each side were open, revealing tantalizing glimpses of the delights inside—or the horrors, depending on which side, literally, you were on.

To the right, the smaller of the two galleries—another bone of contention—was devoted to representational paintings, punctuated by the occasional marble portrait bust or piece of bronze garden statuary. To the left, the larger room held the big, bold canvases and sculptures made of welded metal, found objects, and other unconventional materials that prompted the traditionalists to utter those well-worn phrases.

In search of the Pollock painting they had been told would be there, the Fitzgeralds turned left. It was immediately obvious why the abstractionists had been given the larger room—some of their things were enormous. Sprawling along one wall was Ossorio's four-part construction, its sections joined by copper piping and decorated with lively swirling threads of black paint over multicolored backgrounds. James Brooks's piece was a scroll-like canvas, some eight feet long, into which he had soaked diluted paint instead of brushing it on. In fact the image was actually the back of the canvas, not the painted side. His wife, Charlotte Park, had submitted a more modestly scaled effort, a mere five by four feet, in oil paint applied with brushes in the traditional way, which was nonetheless just as abstract, equally improvisational, and even more colorful.

Bracketed by a dynamic Lee Krasner collage, nearly seven feet tall, composed of shredded canvas and black photographer's backdrop paper on top of one of her recycled 1951 paintings, and an even taller abstraction of energetically brushed, fragmented forms by Willem de Kooning—Pollock's Springs neighbor, drinking buddy, and rival for the title of America's Number One Action Painter—was the Pollock. Whoever had hung the exhibition, which opened the day before the accident, must now be aware of the irony of that juxtaposition, as was nearly everyone who saw it. On one side of the Pollock was the heir to his legacy, and on the other, the inheritor of his mantle.

The canvas itself, titled *Search,* was modest by Pollock standards—only about five by seven feet—but it overflowed with the turbulent energy for which he was famous. After years of simply numbering his paintings he had recently gone back to naming them at the request of his dealer, Sidney Janis, who had a hard time keeping track of the inventory, since the artist started a new *Number 1* each year. And titles, Janis had persuaded him, made the paintings easier to sell.

Search was dated 1955. Although most exhibition-goers didn't know it, this was the last canvas Pollock had ever painted, more than a year earlier.

As they had been when confronted with *Number 1, 1950* at The Creeks, Fitz and Nita were initially perplexed, and they were not alone. Another couple was also pondering the composition, an amalgam of several techniques, each vying for dominance. Areas of raw canvas were stained with thinned black enamel, a tactic Pollock had pioneered and Brooks had adopted. Touches of brushed-on green danced around the edges and filled in some of the gaps, while others were in-painted with a rusty red that looked disconcertingly like blood. The whole thing was overlaid with blotches of thick white oil paint that appeared to have been applied straight from the tube. Desultory trickles of black enamel had been poured on top, almost like an afterthought. It seemed that *Search* was an apt name for it.

"I don't understand the title, much less the picture itself," said the man to his wife. "What's it supposed to mean?"

"What does it mean to you?" came a youthful but confident voice, and the couple turned to find that their questioner was an eight-year-old boy, who was about to give them an art appreciation lesson.

FORTY-SIX.

Before returning to the cottage, Fitz and Nita decided to pay a call on Chief Steele in the hope that Hector Morales had nailed Petrillo. Unfortunately the news was not good, except for Petrillo.

"His blood doesn't match," they were told, "and in any case Hector found no wounds on him. I'm afraid we're stymied."

"With Pollock out of the running," said Fitz, "if it's not someone who had a personal connection to Metzger, like Kligman and Petrillo, or one of Krasner's sympathizers, it could be a total stranger who just happened on her in the dark and assaulted her, maybe tried to rape her and got scared off when she started to choke. Either a local or a transient who's long gone and we may never be able to identify."

"There's only one way to move this thing along," Nita proposed, "and that's to make the information about the skin fragments public. If we let it be known that Metzger's killer can be identified by claw marks and a matching blood type, maybe we can flush him out. Especially if it's someone from around here."

Considering his brief but revealing experience with the local community, Fitz had a very pertinent question. "Would the Bonackers turn in one of their own?"

Steele took his time answering. "That's a hard call. They're a self-protective bunch that don't take kindly to snitches. They perfected the code of silence during Prohibition, when the rumrunners were the backbone of the Bonac economy, but I think they'd draw the line at harboring a killer. If we follow Nita's advice, I guess we'll find out."

"I don't think Mike would keep quiet if he thought somebody he knew was guilty," said TJ. Evidently the Collins boy had confided to him that he and Jackson were pals, and that he was really broken up about his death. "Right now everybody thinks Jackson killed her, so he'd want to clear his buddy's name."

"That's a good point, TJ," said Steele. "Well, I'd better set the wheels in motion. Can't wait for the next edition of the *Star*, so we'll have to rely on word of mouth. And I know just the mouth." He flipped on the intercom and buzzed the clerk out front.

"Fred, I've got a job for you. Get on the horn to Millie over at the Sea Spray. Tell her you just found out that Metzger wounded her killer and the cops are looking for a man with deep scratches on his face or arms. Tell her Pollock's definitely been eliminated. Don't say anything about the blood type, just the claw marks from Metzger's fingernails. No such marks on Pollock, you can tell her."

He flipped off the intercom. "In case you haven't actually met her in person, Millie Dayton is the Sea Spray's switchboard operator. That news will be all over Bonac before dinnertime, I guarantee."

FORTY-SEVEN.

Saturday, August 18

With Jackson Pollock's last will and testament in hand, Gerard Weinstock, Esq., knocked on Lee's door at eleven a.m. He had driven out the evening before, directly from the office, but waited until he'd had a good night's sleep and a hearty breakfast before confronting her. He had a pretty clear idea what she was going to propose.

Under the terms of the will, Lenore Krasner Pollock was Jackson's sole heir and executrix. Not only did she inherit his entire estate, but she also had exclusive and absolute control over its disposition. Lee had persuaded Jackson that she was the only one who could be relied on to act in the best interests of his legacy, and he had gone along with her.

In spite of Weinstock's expressed disapproval, there were no bequests to anyone else, which was bound to cause resentment when the will was made public. Adding insult to injury, in a codicil Jackson authorized Lee to lend (not give) some of his paintings to his brothers, leaving to her discretion which paintings (maybe none) and for how long (maybe never). There was no question in Weinstock's mind that these terms would anger the Pollock family.

There was, however, an alternative provision in case Lee predeceased Jackson, or for some reason failed to qualify as his executrix. Jackson had insisted that if either of those things happened, his brother Sanford was to be the executor. But Lee had survived to inherit it all, and she wanted to move as quickly as possible to make her own will, one guaranteeing that no one in the Pollock clan would ever get posthumous control of Jackson's estate.

As much as she understood the wisdom—indeed, as she saw it, the necessity—of doing this, it was causing her deep emotional anxiety. Writing a will meant acknowledging one's mortality. Back in 1951 it had been hard enough for her to face the possibility of Jackson's death, but it had been brought home to her when he fell off the wagon and couldn't get back on. Without Dr. Heller to turn to, he had floundered.

When she realized she was losing him, she vowed she would not lose the paintings into which he had poured so much of himself. They meant more to her than financial security, far more.

She answered her attorney's knock in a bathrobe and slippers. She had never been an early riser, though compared to Jackson, who hardly ever saw the morning, she

was up with the sun. Today, dreading yet another diffi-
cult and painful chore, she was having a hard time getting
started.

Before she could apologize or even greet him, Weinstock
wrapped his arms around her with heartfelt sympathy.

"I'm so sorry, Lee, so sorry," he whispered as she re-
ciprocated, letting herself be comforted as much by his
reassuring presence as by his embrace.

"I thought you'd never get here," she scolded as he
sat down, opened his briefcase, and laid the will on the
kitchen table. "It's been one disaster after another. First
the accident, then the funeral—Mags has probably told
you all about that—then the story in the paper about the
Metzger woman being dead before the crash. Have you
seen last Thursday's *Star*?" Weinstock said yes, his wife
had shown it to him.

"Thank God they're not blaming Jackson for that."

"Really? How so? From what the paper said, it seems . . ."

"Yes, doesn't it? What other conclusion would you
draw? But Harry Steele says he's ruled out Jackson as the
killer." She couldn't resist turning the chief's report from
provisional to definite.

Weinstock asked the obvious question. "If Jackson
didn't do it, who did?"

"The investigation is in progress, that's all I know.
Harry said he'd keep me informed. Meanwhile I have
more important things to think about, namely the will,
or rather wills. Jackson's and mine."

"I've already submitted Jackson's for probate. I have to warn you, it could take a while. The art will have to be appraised, and there will be tax liabilities and other financial obligations. I'll defer my fee until the estate is settled, and it will be nominal.

"Now, as to your will, if you hadn't suggested making one right away I would have recommended it. The terms of Jackson's will, naming you as sole heir, are now in force." He opened the document and pointed out the provision he wanted to discuss. "But without your own will, if you should, ah, cease to be a qualified executrix, Jackson's brother Sande would take over, and I know you don't want that."

"Damn right I don't," said Lee emphatically. "He has no idea how to manage Jackson's legacy. The paintings would just be meal tickets to him. He'd sell them off to anyone, just to get enough money to put his brats through school, maybe hire somebody to run that crummy print shop of his."

"People fall ill, accidents happen. If, God forbid, you were to pass away intestate, Sande would inherit."

"Exactly, and that's not going to happen. I want my brother, Irving, to handle the estate if, for whatever reason, I can't. He understands what's involved, and I trust him completely."

"Have you discussed this with him?"

"Yes. We had dinner together in the city on Thursday night, and he agreed."

Weinstock was making notes on a yellow legal pad. "He lives in Brooklyn, doesn't he? Let me have his address and phone numbers, home and office, please." He wrote down the information. "I'll get in touch with him and arrange a meeting among the three of us at my office. Meanwhile I'll draft something for you both to review before we meet." He stood, and she walked with him to the door.

"By the way," he remarked as he prepared to leave, "I saw your brother last Saturday night, only in passing. I didn't recognize him at first—hadn't seen him in a while—and by the time I realized who it was he was gone."

"You mean in the city?" said Lee, assuming they'd bumped into each other on the street. "I thought you and the family were out here last weekend."

"It *was* out here," he explained. "Mags and the kids have been here since the beginning of August, but I've only been able to get away at the weekends. Last week I was preparing for a big court case—the one that kept me away from the funeral—and I had to spend Saturday at the office. I knew I'd be late, so I took the car in, grabbed a bite after work, and hit the road around seven.

"When I got to East Hampton I decided to gas up, so I pulled into that all-night filling station on the highway, just outside town. There was a car in front of me at the pump. I wasn't paying much attention, but I saw the driver come out of the men's room. He was holding a handkerchief to his face, so I couldn't see who he was at first, but he took his hand down when he paid for the gas and I recognized Irving."

Lee was incredulous. "Are you sure, Gerry? Absolutely certain?"

"He was standing right under the light. I started to get out of the car to say hi, but he hopped into his car and pulled away before I could. He was in a hurry."

"But he doesn't own a car," she told him. "He used to have one, but he sold it last year. And what the hell would he be doing in East Hampton all alone on a Saturday night? You must have been mistaken."

Even as she spoke those words, Lee got an inkling of something amiss.

"What is it, Lee? Are you all right?" She had sat back down at the table and was looking off into space, focusing on something far away.

"I'm fine, Gerry, just confused. I don't know what to think. I'll have to ask him. Or maybe he has a double out here. You've got me all muddled."

"Why don't you call him? I'm sure there's an explanation."

"Of course," she said, a bit vaguely. "That's just what I'm going to do."

FORTY-EIGHT.

Fred Tucker greeted his boss with a hearty "'Morning, Chief," as Steele entered the station promptly at nine a.m. "Got a bite on your line already."

"You don't say? Boy, that was quick. What's the story?"

"Charlie Osborne, the gas jockey over at Pratt's Tydol station on the highway, called in to say he saw somebody with a face wound last Saturday night. Wants to give you the details in person."

"Is he on the job now?"

"No, he works six to midnight on weekends. Says you'll find him at home this morning." Fred gave him the address, which was, not surprisingly, on Osborne Lane.

"Any other tips?" asked Steele as he prepared to call on Charlie.

"Not yet, but Millie only got the word out yesterday afternoon. Not everybody has heard yet."

"You know better than that, Fred. There's not a body

aboveground anywhere in this town who doesn't know what we're lookin' for by now."

It was a short drive down Newtown Lane to the Osborne Lane turnoff, then almost as far as Cedar Street to Charlie's house, number 84. Three decades ago Steele would have ridden there on his Indian motorcycle, cutting a dashing figure as the first—and only—member of the East Hampton Town police force. Now, nearing retirement, and with the Indian up on blocks in the garage, he was content to sit behind the wheel of his comfortable 1955 Ford Fairlane Crown Victoria, a recent acquisition that signaled his superior status.

As Steele pulled the patrol car into the driveway, Charlie Osborne came out to meet him. A senior at East Hampton High School, he had a summer job at Pratt's Service Station, which kept the gas pumps open all night during the summer season.

"Thanks for droppin' by, Chief," said Charlie with a handshake. "I called as soon as I heard the news."

"When was that?" Steele wanted to know.

"Over breakfast," the young man replied. "Ma heard it last night from Mrs. Edwards down street. I 'spect she woulda told me right then, only she was asleep by the time I got off work. I do the late shift from Friday to Sunday nights. Actually Ma thought maybe it was just a rumor, 'cause everybody was sure Pollock done it, what with her bein' in his car. But I said wait a minute, maybe there's somethin' to it."

"What makes you think that?"

"Come up on the porch and set while I give you the scoop," said Charlie, and the two men retired to a matching pair of rockers.

"You know Friday's the busiest night," Charlie began, "with all the city folks headed out here wantin' to gas up for the weekend. And Sunday they're all goin' in the opposite direction, gassin' up again for the trip back, so that's pretty busy, too. Plenty of out-of-town plates pullin' in and out all night.

"Saturday night's a lot quieter, mostly local customers, a few day-trippers on the way home. Last Saturday, a little after ten it was, a guy pulls up to the pump and asks where the men's room is. He's holdin' a hankie to his cheek, and it's soaked with blood. 'That's a nasty cut,' I says, and he says, 'Yeah, I fell in the parking lot, right on my face. I need to clean it up.' So I point him to the john and ask if he wants gas. He says sure, fill 'er up, but don't bother with under the hood 'cause he's in a rush, and anyway it's a rental."

"Do you remember which cheek?"

"The left one, on the window side. Anyway, I pumped the gas while he was in the john. When he came out he was still holdin' the hankie on his face, but it looked like he'd washed it out and soaked it in cold water. When he took his hand down to pay me, I got a good look at the damage. He had two nasty scratches right across his cheek, like this." Charlie ran his fingertips along his cheekbone.

"I told him she took six gallons and he owed me a buck fifty. He handed me two bucks and said to keep the change. That's another reason I remember him—not many city folks are good tippers."

"How do you know he was from the city?"

"His plates. They had a KN prefix, that's Kings County—Brooklyn. I don't remember the numbers, but he said it was a rental, so it shouldn't be too hard to trace. He wasn't kiddin' when he said he was in a hurry. He pulled out real quick and gunned it, goin' west, to my surprise."

"How so?"

"The only strangers headed west on a Saturday night are the day-trippers, almost always fishermen with tackle or families who been to the beach or the farm stands, so their cars're loaded with stuff. His car had nothin' in it but him, and he was wearin' city clothes, not country casual. Looked more like a businessman than a tourist."

Steele complimented Osborne on his excellent memory and remarkable eye for detail. "You're on the ball, Charlie. If I ever get the budget for a detective, you should definitely apply."

FORTY-NINE.

"Hello, Izzy, it's Lee. I just had a meeting with Gerry about the will, and he told me something that surprised and confused me."

After Weinstock left, she had gone straight to the phone. Fortunately her brother was at home, so she didn't have to spend hours wondering why he had told her that he couldn't get to East Hampton until Sunday and that there was no longer any point in going after he heard about the car crash from Alfonso.

"I thought the terms of Jackson's will were clear," Irving replied. "Was there some problem with the wording? It's not like Gerry to leave anything ambiguous or open to interpretation."

"No, no, nothing like that." She was hesitant, trying to figure out how to phrase the question.

"Was he unfavorable to the idea of my taking over the Pollock estate in case of your death or disability? You told him I had agreed, didn't you? Surely he wouldn't object to that."

"No, of course not. It's not about Jackson's will, or mine." Better just put it out there and see what he says.

"Izzy, were you in East Hampton last Saturday?"

The question was met with a momentary silence. He certainly was not prepared for it. How could she possibly know? He decided to obfuscate.

"What makes you think I was?"

"Gerry says he saw you."

Impossible. Only two people had seen him face-to-face, and Weinstock wasn't one of them. And the two who did see him didn't know him from Adam.

"He must have seen someone who looks like me." Evasive, but not a bald-faced lie. He was playing for time.

"That's what I told him," said Lee, "but he insisted it was you. He said you were at the filling station when he pulled in to get gas. You were in the car ahead of him."

Irving's mind was in turmoil. *Jesus fucking Christ, of all the rotten coincidences, how improbable is that one? Yes, there was a car behind me, but what were the chances that the guy in it was someone who knew me? Late at night on the highway, in a town I hardly ever visit, that was the last thing I would have expected.*

"I'm sorry to contradict Gerry, but he's wrong. I told you I couldn't get a rental car on Saturday, so how could I have been buying gas in East Hampton that night?"

Now it was Lee's turn to go silent. She hadn't mentioned the time of day Gerry said he saw her brother. She felt a little stab of pain in her chest as the implication registered. Still, she couldn't bring herself to confront it directly.

"You couldn't, could you? Not without a car, obviously. I guess Gerry was imagining things. He did say it was quite late, and he'd driven all the way out from the city and was probably tired. I guess that explains it."

Irving sounded relieved. "That's right. Just a case of mistaken identity. Happens all the time. You'd be surprised how often."

After she hung up, Lee retreated to the kitchen for more coffee, cigarettes, and mental turbulence. As if she didn't have enough to deal with, she now had to confront the likelihood that her brother, her most trusted ally and emotional lifeline, had lied to her. That he had come out on Saturday after all. That he needed to deny it, but why? He had been so insistent that she still held out hope he was telling the truth and it was all a mistake. As of now she only had Gerry's word for it. If she could confirm his story, if anyone else had seen Izzy, then at least she would know for sure. She decided to call around.

It was a fruitless exercise. None of her friends had seen him since earlier in the summer, before she left for Europe. He didn't come out often, since he and Jackson didn't get along, and when he did show up it was usually because Lee was at her wit's end and needed someone to run interference for her.

His presence had a salutary effect on Jackson, who was a bit afraid of him. Even though Irving was sixteen years older and going to pot around the middle, he was taller by a couple of inches and built like a wrestler. In his condition Jackson was no match for him and he knew it.

He could brawl with his artist friends, since they pulled their punches and it was all in good fun, but with Irving it would be serious, so when he was around, Jackson steered clear of any confrontation, spending most of the time in his studio, out with the dogs, or over at the General Store shooting the breeze with Dan Miller and drinking beer with his Bonacker buddies. But he'd been avoiding them lately, not wanting them to see how frail he was, physically and emotionally.

And besides, once Lee was out of the picture he had Ruth to keep him occupied.

FIFTY.

Gerry Weinstock returned to the family's summer cottage on the other side of Fireplace Road to find his wife and children piling beach chairs, inner tubes, pails, shovels, towels, and a folding sunshade into the Packard. With a large lunch basket already stocked and waiting on the kitchen table, he didn't have to ask where they were going, or for how long.

The beach at nearby Louse Point was a family favorite. With a long, shallow slope out into Gardiner's Bay, no rough waves or undertow, the water was perfect for youngsters. Margaret was sure to find other mothers to gossip with, and the kids would have lots of playmates.

"Coming with us, Gerry?" she called as he entered the kitchen. "I've packed plenty of food." He joined her at the table, where she was filling the Thermos with lemonade. He caressed her cheek and kissed her, just warmly enough to distract her while he stole a cookie from the pile she was about to wrap.

"Naughty boy, you'll spoil your lunch," she scolded, grinning indulgently. "Now get changed if you're coming."

"I think I'll skip the beach today, Mags," he said. "I want to make a few notes after my conversation with Lee. She wants me to draw up her will, and it needs to be done right away to protect her interests. I should get on it while the terms she wants are fresh in my mind."

Margaret was disappointed, but inclined to be sympathetic to Lee's demands on her husband's time and attention. "I understand, Gerry. My heart goes out to her. She must be going through hell emotionally, losing Jackson in such a terrible way, and then that girl's murder on top of it. At least Jackson's been cleared of that."

"How do you know?"

"Well, I was over at the General Store getting some stuff for lunch, and Mrs. Collins was in there, talking to Dan. She said the police have ruled out Jackson as the killer. Apparently the poor girl struggled with her attacker and scratched him, probably on his face. They found skin under her nails. Jackson didn't have a wound like that, so they're looking for someone else."

Gerry sat down at the table. "A face wound, you say. I wonder . . ."

But in his lawyerly way, and knowing how tales get around, Gerry first needed to check that it wasn't just a rumor. He went to the front hall and telephoned the police station.

Fred Tucker confirmed the story. "That's right, Mr.

Weinstock, we believe Miss Metzger scratched whoever strangled her—most likely a man, but not Mr. Pollock. He had to be strong enough to crush her windpipe, but not before she clawed at him. Most likely got him on the face or neck. That's not consistent with Mr. Pollock's injuries."

But it is consistent with an injury I saw, said Gerry to himself. *And I saw it on the night, and around the time, Edith Metzger died.*

"If it isn't confidential, Mr. Tucker, can you tell me if there are any suspects?"

"I can't say, Mr. Weinstock, but you bein' a family friend, I can tell you that the chief interviewed somebody this morning. Not a suspect, but somebody who may have information."

Gerry paused, then came to a decision. "Is Chief Steele in? I'd like to speak to him."

"No, sir, he's still out. But we have a detective from the city helping us out. She knows the details. I'll ask her to call you."

"Thank you, Mr. Tucker. I'll be at home." He gave the clerk his number.

Instead of returning directly to the station, Harry Steele had decided to report his findings to the Fitzgeralds. Once again he caught them finishing a leisurely breakfast and planning a day out. They had only three more left before their vacation ended and they returned to the city on Tuesday.

"I'm not gonna keep you," he told them, "but I could use your advice about a new development. The bait landed us a fish, and I'm hoping to reel him in. Only first I have to find out what kind of fish he is."

"You're being very cryptic," said Fitz, "and I wouldn't know a cod from a catfish, but if we can help, just say the word."

Steele recounted his interview with Charlie Osborne.

"I'll tell you, that boy's got the sharpest eyes in town. He even got a partial on the license plate. Do you think you could have someone at your precinct check the car rental places in Brooklyn? Just call around and see who booked a car last Saturday?"

"Sure," said Fitz. "Can't be too many outfits, they're probably all in the Yellow Pages. Only problem would be if it's just a local garage, or if he rented it for more than one day—in other words, he already had it before Saturday and didn't turn it in right away. But we'll start with the assumption that it was a rental agency and a one-day deal and see if we get lucky."

He went inside and emerged with some change for the pay phone. "I wouldn't want Millie Dayton spreading this around," he remarked. "She's a pretty effective broadcaster."

Steele chuckled. "You're not kiddin'. But I told Mrs. Pollock the good news myself. Didn't want her learnin' it secondhand. And she's had enough bad news to last her a lifetime."

"That was thoughtful," said Nita. Even though she'd never met the woman, and had heard enough about her to form a somewhat negative opinion, she hated to think of her dealing with the possibility that her late husband was a murderer.

"I'll have the clerk call you directly," Fitz told Steele. "No need to go through me. Besides, we can't hang around here all day. TJ wants to go on a fishing expedition of his own, a real one. We're thinking of driving out to Montauk and renting a boat and some tackle so all three of us can try our luck."

"Well," said Steele rather sheepishly. "I hate to delay your family outing, but I wasn't to ask Nita another favor." A collective groan went up from the Fitzgeralds. "Maybe it won't take all that long," he added. "I got a radio call from Fred that a city fella named Gerard Weinstock wants to talk to me, and maybe has some information about the case. I thought Nita might talk to him instead."

"Of course," Nita replied. "I'll go to the pay phone with Fitz." Steele gave her the number and said he'd wait for her report.

"You'll be on your way to Montauk in no time," he assured them. "Gosman's Dock will have everything you need. Tell Bob Gosman I sent you. That way he'll charge you the local price."

"Thank you for calling, Detective Diaz," Gerry began. He recognized her name from the article in the *Star*. "I understand you're helping out with the Metzger investigation. I'm an attorney. Lee Pollock is one of my clients, as well as a neighbor in Springs. That's how I met her and Jackson. My family has a place almost opposite theirs on Fireplace Road. Over the years we've become good friends, and I wrote Jackson's last will and testament. Lee and I had a conference this morning about the estate, and something came up that prompted my call to Chief Steele."

Nita detected the hesitancy in Weinstock's voice. "How's that, sir?"

"It's a bit awkward, considering my close personal and professional relationship with Lee. It would be helpful if you could share some information about your latest line of inquiry. About the search for a suspect other than Jackson, I mean. My wife heard about it this morning, and she told me."

"What kind of information?"

"Do you have a line on anyone?"

He knows something, guessed Nita, *or thinks he might.* Her years of experience had given her a keen ear for hidden meanings. She decided to draw Weinstock out.

"It's possible we do, Mr. Weinstock. As you must have heard, we haven't much to go on, only the assumption that the killer was wounded in a certain way. We think he was scratched on the face. It seems a man answering that description was seen around the time in question."

"What time was that?"

"A little after ten last Saturday night."

"Have you identified the man?"

Nita laid her cards on the table. "Can you help us with that, sir?"

Weinstock was taken aback. Had he been so transparent? Apparently he had. He felt like one of the mercenary clients he walked through the intricacies of contracts, wills, and other complex legal agreements, probing their motives until they admitted to hidden agendas. But he was not about to drop his professional discretion.

"As I said, I'm in an awkward position. My client's interests come first, and I need to consider how best they may be served. Please answer another question for me."

"If I can without compromising the investigation," Nita replied.

"Where was the suspect seen?"

"Pratt's Service Station on Montauk Highway."

Gerry's heart sank. "Thank you, Detective Diaz. I appreciate your being so forthcoming. I need to verify something, and I'll report back as soon as possible." He rang off.

The suspicion that had been nagging at him since he spoke to Fred Tucker had been confirmed.

FIFTY-ONE.

He tried phoning Lee, but the line was busy. He decided to walk across—better to talk to her in person anyway. It was not going to be an easy conversation.

He found her in the front parlor, wearing a housedress now but still in her slippers, sitting at the table with her address book on the blotter next to the phone. She had been working her way through it in an effort to find out if anyone had seen Irving on Saturday, which is why the line was perpetually engaged.

More than one of her friends had told her the news of Jackson's exoneration, so it was clear that the word had spread widely.

When she saw Weinstock come through the back door she waved him in.

"I knew Jackson couldn't have done it," she declared with satisfaction. "I refused to believe it, and I was right." She hadn't been all that sure in the beginning, but any misgivings she'd had were now gone.

Gerry took the wing chair next to the table and reached out his hand to Lee in a gesture of reassurance. She grasped it firmly.

"I'm going to be all right now, Gerry. I've accepted Jackson's death as inevitable. It wouldn't have mattered whether I was here or not—in my heart I know that. I can't forgive him for cheating on me, at least not yet, perhaps I will in time. He was a desperate man, and deeply disturbed. That psychiatrist wasn't helping him at all. Anyway, it's over now, and while I can't defend his behavior at least I know he didn't kill someone else, only himself."

"Your attitude does you great credit, Lee. You did everything you could for Jackson. It's not your fault that it wasn't enough."

She's trying to put it behind her, he thought, *but she's much more fragile than she lets on. There's more tragedy to come. And I'm the one who has to lay it at her doorstep.*

"You do realize," he began, "that with Jackson in the clear, someone else killed Edith Metzger."

"Of course. Isn't that the point? I expect the police will figure it out."

"I had a talk with the police, and I understand they have a suspect."

Lee gasped. "My God, Gerry, that's wonderful! Did he tell you who it is?"

"They don't have a name, just a description, and a witness. Actually there may be two witnesses." He paused, then withdrew his hand from hers. "I think I'm one of them."

Lee's brow furrowed. "What the hell do you mean?"

Then her expression changed as she put two and two together. Gerry's story about the gas station. The promise to take care of Ruth. The cheek wound—she'd seen it in the city. Not Jackson after all. Her worst fear realized.

She stiffened, and closed her eyes tight.

"Oh, no, Gerry. I couldn't stand it. Please tell me it's a mistake."

"I hope to God it is, but he'll have to be questioned, Lee. I haven't said anything to Steele yet, but I can't withhold evidence."

She was crumbling before his eyes. Not hysterical, not raging—those reactions seemed to have been all used up on Jackson. This time she was imploding. Suddenly she groaned and doubled over with a cramp, almost hitting her head on the table.

He jumped to her side, put his arms around her, and helped her up. "Mags has the car or I'd drive you to the doctor," he told her. "You need something to help you get through this. Here, lie down on the couch while I call Alfonso. He'll come pick you up." He steered her to the sofa, settled her, and stepped across the room to the phone.

It took Ossorio only fifteen minutes to arrive. Weinstock hadn't given him the details, only said that Lee had taken a bad turn and needed a sedative.

First he had called Dr. Abel's office. The doctor was in all afternoon on Saturdays in the summer, when a parade of casualties—from fingers impaled by fishhooks to bicycle mishaps and children hit by softballs or fallen out of trees or bitten by the swans in Town Pond—attested to the haplessness of city folk. And he was always braced for a drowning or another car crash. He said he could see Lee right away.

One on either side, they took her into the office. She was silent and uncharacteristically passive, allowing herself to be supported and led. Fortunately there was no one in the waiting room, and the receptionist sent them straight in. They left her in the doctor's care and said they'd wait in the car. Weinstock wanted to brief Ossorio in private.

"Unbelievable" was the response. "Why would he do such a thing? It makes no sense at all."

"That was my initial reaction," said Weinstock. "I doubted myself, just as I doubt all eyewitness accounts in court because I know how unreliable they are. But I'm sure of what I saw, and it fits with what Detective Diaz told me. Someone else saw him at the filing station, too—she didn't say, but it must have been the attendant. Of course he's unlikely to have known who he was, but he could give a good description.

"Now I've had time to think it through, I can see what might have happened. It's a case of mistaken identity, all right, but not on my part. It was Irving who made the mistake."

FIFTY-TWO.

By the time the Fitzgeralds had returned from Montauk that evening, toting a haul of bluefish that Nita now knew how to prepare, plus salad fixings and a peach pie from the farm stand in Amagansett, the investigation had progressed rapidly. After they got cleaned up, Nita volunteered to phone the station from the pay phone for an update.

"We've got evidence from two directions," Steele told her, "out here and in the city. The clerk at the Sixth Precinct traced the rental car. It came from Hertz on Atlantic Avenue in Brooklyn. Customer booked it for Saturday morning, but the previous customer didn't return it until late that afternoon. All their other cars were out and they had to clean it, so the guy couldn't pick it up until nearly seven p.m. He paid cash, said he'd have it back Sunday morning. They remembered him real well, because he called every hour to find out if it was ready."

"How do you know it's our guy?"

"Because when he filled up on the way back to Brooklyn, he was spotted by someone who recognized him. A positive ID that matches the name on the rental."

"Well, who is it?"

"Mr. Irving Krasner."

"*¡Que me aspen!* I mean, I'll be darned. What relation is he to Lee?"

"Her brother. He lives at 1630 80th Street in Bensonhurst, an easy subway ride to the Hertz office. It was his bad luck that Lee's lawyer, Gerry Weinstock, decided to fill up his gas tank at the same time at Pratt's Tydol station on the highway. Weinstock saw him, and saw the scratches on his face. When he found out we were looking for someone of that description, he felt obliged to come forward. He called us about an hour after you left for Montauk.

"He broke it to Lee first, and she took it hard. Mind you, it's not air-tight yet, and we don't know why he did it, though Weinstock has a theory."

"Which is?"

"He thought she was Ruth Kligman."

"You mean he came out here to kill Ruth and got the wrong girl?"

"Not exactly. According to Weinstock's reasoning, Lee found out that Kligman had moved in with Pollock and sent her brother to break it up. You remember Ruth said Edith wasn't in the house when they came down, and the back door was open. She must have gone outside, and when Irving showed up and found her out there in the dark he assumed she was the girl he was after. He'd never seen her before, and how was he to know there were *two* of them there that weekend?"

"I see where this is leading," said Nita. "Irving says you're leaving right now and tries to force her into the car. Edith has no idea who he is, thinks he's trying to rape her, and puts up a fight. Maybe she starts to scream, so he grabs her by the throat. She flails at him and scratches his face, which makes him see red and squeeze too hard. He panics and beats it."

"That's pretty much the way Weinstock figured it. And it fits with Kligman's account, how she and Pollock came out and found her lying in the yard gasping for breath." Nita nodded in agreement.

"I called back to the Sixth Precinct and asked if they could get someone to go around to Krasner's place and question him," Steele continued. "Get a blood sample, too. They put the local Brooklyn precinct on it and they hauled him in for questioning. He didn't admit anything, but they got him to agree to photos and a blood sample. We can't receive photos by wire, so they're sending them out on the train. Should be here at six fifty-seven, if she's on time. Front and both profiles, plus a close-up of the wound on his face. It's almost healed, but the Brooklyn cop said it's two clear scratches on his left cheek. Finch can run the pictures over to Pratt's—that's the filling station—and show them to the Charlie."

"What about the blood? Have they typed it?"

"They sure have. Irving Krasner is A positive. A perfect match."

Over beers for herself and Fitz and a Hires root beer for TJ, Nita filled them in on the latest news.

"Looks like they collared him," said Fitz with satisfaction. "Shows you how teamwork really pays off."

Nita agreed. "Even without Osborne's identification they have enough evidence for an arrest warrant. After all, Weinstock saw him, too, and he knows him. It's circumstantial—just because he was out here at the right time doesn't make him guilty—but it's pretty damning, especially with the scratches and matching blood type."

"I'm glad it wasn't Ted or Alfonso," said TJ. "They're great guys, even if they are pansies."

Fitz chuckled. "Takes all kinds, buddy. Remember that when you're pounding the beat. It helps to be broad-minded."

Nita, eyes narrowed, gazed sternly at her husband. "Don't you go giving him ideas, Brian Francis Xavier Fitzgerald. Maybe the force isn't for him. How do you know he doesn't want to be a doctor, like Bill Abel, or a lawyer, like Gerry Weinstock? What do you think, *Juanito?*"

"I think I want to be an artist, like Jackson Pollock" was his answer, causing both parents to threaten to disown him, put him up for adoption, or send him to military school. Or all three.

FIFTY-THREE.

Saturday, November 2, 1957

Harry Steele's retirement party was held at the Huntting Inn on Main Street. Unlike the Sea Spray, which closed after Labor Day weekend, this venerable establishment—where grub and grog had been dispensed since 1751—stayed open through the fall.

In his own way Steele was an equally venerated institution. He had inaugurated the East Hampton Town police force thirty-four years earlier, and was being given a splendid send-off by what was now a ten-man department, together with many well-wishers from the community and farther afield, including the Fitzgerald family.

"I hope you invited the local criminals to this shindig," quipped Fitz as he raised his glass in Steele's honor, "'cause the town is completely unprotected today. All the cops are in this room."

"Those who say there's never a policeman around when you want one know exactly where to look," Steele replied. "I think East Hampton can survive a couple of hours without us, and the place is going to have to get used to not having me around."

"You're not leaving town, are you?"

"Oh, no. Me and the missus wouldn't be happy anywhere else. The kids and the grandkids are here, so I can't see us pullin' up stakes. Maybe I'll get the old Indian goin' again, give the patrol cars somethin' to chase in the off season."

"Make us eat your dust, Chief," chimed in Earl Finch, recently promoted to sergeant. He greeted the Fitzgeralds warmly, with a Bonac hello to TJ, now nine.

"Howdy, bub. Good t'see you again. I hardly knew you, you've grown so." He turned to Fitz and Nita. "Stayin' the weekend? If so I hope you'll come up to us for Sunday lunch. Grace and I would love to have you," he winked at TJ, "and Sally's waitin' to see you. She hasn't helped solve any more crimes since last summer, but she's got another litter of pups." That news got a string of Spanish from TJ, which Nita roughly translated as "Hot diggety!"

Just then TJ saw the Collins family come in. "Hey, Dad," he asked, "can I go say hi to my buddy Mike?" His father excused him and off he went.

"I like a city fella who doesn't forget his Bonac buddies," said Finch. "Finest kind. I'm sure glad you folks can stay over."

"Alfonso and Ted are putting us up at The Creeks," said Nita. "Ted and TJ spent the afternoon in the kitchen, whipping up a batch of bread. Our boy is learning some very useful culinary skills."

"He was my sous-chef for the *coq au vin* we're having for dinner tonight," said Ted, who had arrived on cue. "Mind you, I think we'll have to hold it over 'til Sunday. No one is going to leave here hungry." The inn had laid on a lavish buffet, as well as an open bar that put everyone in a nostalgic frame of mind. They couldn't help but look back on the previous year, and the circumstances that had brought them together.

"Compared to 'fifty-six, your last year on the job must have been like a victory lap," observed Nita. "Not a single murder since then, so they tell me."

"Well, legally speaking, the Metzger killing wasn't murder," Steele reminded her. "Gerry Weinstock felt so bad about being the one to finger Irving Krasner that he really went to bat for him. He's not a criminal lawyer, but he recommended a great one—and I think he paid the bill."

"That's what I heard," Fitz interjected. "The guy got Krasner to take a plea of involuntary manslaughter and waive a jury trial. He figured a jury wouldn't be sympathetic to a guy who killed a refugee from Nazi Germany, even though both he and the victim were Jewish."

Steele took up the story. "It was a winning strategy, and Krasner's confession read pretty much like Weinstock had figured it. He thought she was Ruth, and was just trying to get her away from Jackson. Certainly didn't intend to do her in. In fact he didn't even realize he'd killed her until he read the *Post* on the Friday. They picked up the *Star* story about her being strangled. Considering the circumstances, the judge took it easy on him. So Krasner's doing only two to five up in Wallkill. Probably be out in less than two if he plays by the rules."

"And for the rest of his life he'll have to live with his guilt," said Fitz. "Sadly, so will his sister. How's she doing, by the way?"

Ted's admiration was enthusiastic. "That woman is a survivor! After Irving's arrest we feared for her sanity. Her close friends rallied 'round and got her through the worst of it. But she pulled herself together after the sentencing and spent the winter in the city taking care of estate business. We thought she might sell the Springs place, with all its unhappy memories, but back she went this summer and just moved right into Jackson's studio as if it had always been hers.

"Of course it was the smartest thing she could have done. Stake a claim and assert her independence. She hadn't painted in a year, but starting over in that space—so much bigger than the little bedroom studio she had in the house—it was like a rebirth. You should see the work she did! Big, bright, colorful paintings, just gorgeous, nothing like the gloomy things she was doing before. The ghosts were exorcised. We were flabbergasted.

"On top of that," Ted continued, "she's just gotten a huge windfall. Sidney Janis, that super salesman, has persuaded the Metropolitan Museum to pay thirty thousand dollars for a big Pollock called *Autumn Rhythm*. It set a price record for an American painting. Only a couple of years ago the Modern could have snapped it up for eight thousand, but they didn't bite. How ironic that it went to the Met, not exactly a bastion of the avant-garde. Back in 1950 Jackson and his pals lodged a public protest against that old mausoleum for not showing modern art—in other words, *their* art. How's that for a turnabout? And Lee's the one who reaps the reward."

"Well, she deserves it," said Cile, who had joined the group. "She put up with so much of Pollock's horseshit—pardon my language—it's only fair that there really was a pony underneath it." Her new twist on an old joke got a laugh all around.

Ted had more news. "Guess who else is very pleased with herself these days. Ruth Kligman! No sooner was she back on her feet than she was back on her back, this time under Jackson's old nemesis, Bill de Kooning. They've been scorching the sheets since March, just about the one-year anniversary of her hookup with Jackson. Evidently Ruthie's sap rises in the spring."

After many toasts, recaps of highlights from Chief Harry Steele's long and distinguished career, and wishes for his future health and happiness, the party wound down and the guests began to disburse. Friends and acquaintances from the previous year urged Nita, Fitz, and TJ not to be strangers, and return visits were promised.

"Don't forget our lunch date tomorrow," said Finch. "You remember the way, don't you? Up Fireplace Road to Gardiner, turn left, third on the left.

"And take it easy on that curve. It's dangerous."

Patrolman Earl Finch of the East Hampton Town Police with Jackson Pollock's body at the accident scene, August 11, 1956.

PHOTOGRAPH BY DAVE EDWARDES, COURTESY POLLOCK-KRASNER HOUSE AND STUDY CENTER, EAST HAMPTON, NEW YORK. GIFT OF JEFFREY POTTER.

ACKNOWLEDGMENTS

Readers who are familiar with accounts of Jackson Pollock's fatal automobile accident on August 11, 1956, and those who know the history and geography of the Hamptons will recognize many of the people, places, and incidents featured in this book. They won't recognize others, because I made them up.

Brian Fitzgerald and Juanita Diaz are fictional creations of mine. I also invented a few local characters to interact with the real ones involved in the car crash and its aftermath.

Contrary to what I have written, however, Edith Metzger was not strangled by Irving Krasner, who was nowhere near Springs that weekend. She died of a broken neck and head injuries sustained when the car overturned, killing Pollock and seriously injuring Kligman.

My research drew on conversations with some of the real people, most of them now deceased, who appear in this tale—including Paul Brach, who told me the call girl story. The Pollock-Krasner House and Study Center research collections, the East Hampton Library's Long

Island Collection, the *East Hampton Star* digital archives, and Raymond R. Arons's memoir, *The Sea Spray Inn: East Hampton, New York, Summer of 1959*, were invaluable resources.

I also relied heavily on three biographies—*Jackson Pollock: An American Saga* by Steven Naifeh and Gregory White Smith, *To a Violent Grave: An Oral Biography* by Jeffrey Potter, and *Lee Krasner: A Biography* by Gail Levin—as well as Ruth Kligman's book, *Love Affair: A Memoir of Jackson Pollock*. I am grateful to the East Hampton Town Clerk's office for information on the history of the town police, and to Prudence Carabine, née Talmage, a twelfth-generation Bonacker, for preventing me from embarrassing myself regarding the nature and character of her community and its inhabitants.

The Huntting Inn, now a year-round establishment, continues to serve hungry and thirsty travelers, but the Sea Spray burned to the ground in 1978. Its cottages, which now belong to the Village of East Hampton, are still sought-after summer rentals.

Please visit

WWW.DUNEMEREBOOKS.COM

to order your next great read.

DUNEMERE
Books